Wilhelm Rein

The life of Martin Luther

Translated from the German and edited by G.F. Behringer

Wilhelm Rein

The life of Martin Luther
Translated from the German and edited by G.F. Behringer

ISBN/EAN: 9783337126780

Printed in Europe, USA, Canada, Australia, Japan

Cover: Foto ©Raphael Reischuk / pixelio.de

More available books at **www.hansebooks.com**

PREFACE.

THE history of mankind presents us with many great names, but with few great men. And even among those that are called great men, few there are whose records will bear a close scrutiny. In most cases the character of the private man is distinct from the influence of his public career.

Among the immortal names that have honored their kind and glorified their God, stands pre-eminently the name of Martin Luther. Yet not in name alone does his greatness shine forth in splendor after the lapse of four centuries, but in word and deed, in character and influence. His private life and public career are a unit, for both were the manifestations of a sincere soul, a generous heart, a true man.

The enlightened, civilized world celebrates the four hundredth anniversary of this great man's birth. He belongs to the world, to Church and State, for both have felt the influence of his teachings. In the truest estimate of his God-given work he belongs to no sect or party, he is a man of and for the people. In what better way can the memorial of his birth be observed than by a study of his life, his character, and his works ; and above all, by a practical appreciation of the influences which have proceeded from him and blessed mankind ?

To that end this volume has been prepared : to present an attractive life-picture of this representative of the people and servant of God. It is founded upon fact, illustrated from experience, and written for popular comprehension.

In the work of translation and preparation the editor freely consulted and, where necessary, gratefully used, the volumes of Köstlin, Meurer, Krauth, and others, in additions and improvements to the original of Dr. Rein.

But, in the words of Herder, " Of what use to learn of past ages, to praise or to blame ? Let us remember Luther's method of thought, his plain hints and his strong truths, and let us apply them to our own times !" In this spirit this book is sent out on its mission.

G. F. B.

BROOKLYN, October 31, 1883.

CONTENTS.

CHAPTER I.   PAGE

Against Indulgences.......................................   7

CHAPTER II.

Luther's Youth... 17

CHAPTER III.

Luther in the Monastery at Erfurt........................ 27

CHAPTER IV.

Luther as Professor in Wittenberg........................ 36

CHAPTER V.

Luther and the Papal Ambassadors......................... 51

CHAPTER VI.

The Disputation at Leipsic............................... 62

CHAPTER VII.

Concerning the Ban of Excommunication.................... 67

CHAPTER VIII.

Luther Burns the Papal Bull of Excommunication........... 76

CHAPTER IX.

Luther before the Emperor at Worms 82

CHAPTER X.

Luther on the Wartburg................................... 93

CHAPTER XI.

The Troubles at Wittenberg............................... 101

CHAPTER XII.

Luther's Return to Wittenberg............................ 105

CHAPTER XIII.   PAGE

Progress of the Reformation................................ 117

CHAPTER XIV.

Dark Clouds... 124

CHAPTER XV.

Luther's Marriage....................................... 132

CHAPTER XVI.

Luther's Reformatory Activity........................... 136

CHAPTER XVII.

The Conference at Marburg.............................. 151

CHAPTER XVIII.

The Diet at Spire....................................... 158

CHAPTER XIX.

Luther in Coburg Castle................................. 162

CHAPTER XX.

The Diet of Augsburg... 168

CHAPTER XXI.

Until the Death of John the Constant.................... 172

CHAPTER XXII.

Preparations for a Council and Attempts at Union........ 175

CHAPTER XXIII.

Luther in Smalcald..................................... 182

CHAPTER XXIV.

The Closing Years of Luther's Life..................... 186

CHAPTER XXV.

The Death of Martin Luther............................ 192

OPINIONS UPON LUTHER................................ 201

CHRONOLOGICAL TABLE................................. 213

INDEX.. 215

THE LIFE OF MARTIN LUTHER.

CHAPTER I.

AGAINST INDULGENCES.

IT was the 31st of October, 1517. The evening mists had already settled down upon the city of Wittenberg and upon the river Elbe, flowing close by. The city itself was yet alive with activity ; for to-morrow, the first of November, being All Saints' day, would be celebrated as the anniversary of the consecration of the Castle Church. A multitude of people, clergymen and laymen, had congregated in the place. In dense groups they stood along the street leading from the market-place to the castle and awaited the beginning of evening service. But before the bells announced the same, there pressed through the scattered crowds, with rapid strides, an Augustinian monk, pursuing his course directly to the chief entrance of the Castle Church. Here he paused, and drawing from his dark cloak a closely written document, he nailed it to the church door. Then he disappeared within the entrance leading to the sacristy. His act did not excite any particular attention, for it was customary at that time, on the occasion of great festivals, to publish the official announcement of special acts, as well as of university disputations, and to use the church doors for that purpose.

After the monk had disappeared, those standing near
by hastened to the portals of the church. One of the
foremost read the superscription and translated it into
German—for it was written in Latin : " A Disputation
to set forth the Virtue of Indulgences. Actuated by
love and by a desire to bring the truth to light, a disputation will be held at Wittenberg, concerning the following theses, under the direction of the Reverend Father
Martin Luther, Master of the Liberal Arts and of Sacred
Theology, and authorized Teacher of the same. Therefore it is requested, that all who cannot be present in
person to discuss these theses may do so in writing. In
the name of our Lord Jesus Christ. Amen." Scarcely
had the theses, thus published, been read by those nearest
the door, when the evening services began and the multitude poured into the church.

Not long thereafter, the same Augustinian monk that
had nailed the Latin theses to the church door stood in
the pulpit and preached upon the festival text, Luke
19 : 1, etc., which records the history of Zacchæus.
Reverently did the congregation listen to the simple,
calm, and heartfelt sermon of the Augustinian monk.
" Christ must become everything to us," he said ; " and
unto those to whom Christ is something, all else will
be nothing. He must be sought with a heart which,
with a feeling of its unworthiness, does not dare to invite
Him, but which, for that very reason, most urgently
implores His presence. Such a request, coming from
the heart, God will grant. Thus He would have our
hearts. And thus every feast of dedication should not
be merely an outward consecration of a church, but
rather a consecration of the heart unto God." Then
the monk spoke concerning the display of the traffic
with indulgences which was approaching the gates of

Wittenberg. He said but little, however, about this matter, and that without vehemence. "The fault of man," he continued, "to seek his own instead of Christ, and to seek his own even in Christ, is universal; but especially at this time, when seductive preachers of indulgences endeavor to encourage this error." Then he explained to the congregation the difference between spiritual repentance and sacramental repentance, including private confession and church penances. He instructed his hearers that indulgences could refer only to the performance of penance. At the close, he warned them against the error of an imaginary repentance, in feeling sorrow over an imposed penance instead of over the committed sin itself; and that they should not allow themselves to be deceived by the venders of indulgences, so as to be deprived of the salutary effects of punishment in the performance of penance.

This warning against the preachers of indulgences was justified by good reasons. For in the neighborhood of Wittenberg, at the town of Jüterbock, Tetzel, a Dominican monk, carried on his traffic. There were lively times at that place, as at an annual fair and market. The people danced and caroused, rejoicing that they were rid of their sins. And large multitudes flocked from Wittenberg to patronize Tetzel.

The following circumstances led to the traffic in indulgences. The Roman Catholic Church maintained that the saints, during their life on earth, had accumulated a treasury of merit because of their good works; that they had done more good than they were obliged to do. This surplus might be used for the benefit of sinful men who had accomplished less good than was needed for their salvation. The Pope claimed that he had received authority from God to draw from this reservoir of merit, and to apply it to those who had shown themselves worthy by their sorrow and repentance. But soon sorrow and repentance were dispensed with, and matters were satisfactorily arranged by the use of money. Thus arose the so-called traffic in indulgences, which proved to be a source of great revenue to the popes. This was the case under Leo X., who at this time occupied the papal chair. He was a descendant of the famous family of the Medici of Florence. He loved science and art, learning and poetry, as well as splendor and gayety. As for religion, he was not much concerned about it ; for otherwise how could he have used it merely as a source of revenue ?

After the example of his predecessor, Julius II.,* Pope Leo X.† turned the faith of Christian believers in the virtue of indulgences to profitable account by offering this new means of grace for sale, especially in Germany. Resistance to Turkish dominion, which under the powerful influence of the then reigning sultan threatened the overthrow of Christianized Europe, afforded a good pretext. And yet, as touching a war with Turkey, it was a vain pretence. For none of the popes ever seriously entertained this idea, but used it as a cloak to conceal their project of despoiling German lands of their money by means of indulgences. The completion of St. Peter's Church at Rome seems to have been a more serious matter to Pope Leo. In order to acquire the necessary means for this grandest of all buildings in

* Julius II. was born in 1441, and died in 1513. He was chosen Pope in 1503. He laid the corner-stone of St. Peter's Church.

† Leo X. was born in 1475, and died in 1521. He was elected to succeed Julius II. on the 11th of March, 1513. He was ordained a priest March 15th, consecrated a bishop on the 17th, and crowned as Pope on the 19th of March, 1513.

Christendom, he ordered the traffic in indulgences to be carried on with pomp and display. He appointed as the chief business manager of the enterprise Archduke and Archbishop Albert of Mayence, by descent a Prince of Brandenburg, in taste and life a counterpart of the Pope. As a mere youth he was clothed with the high dignity of a triple office as Archbishop of Mayence and Magdeburg, and Bishop of Halberstadt. But this threefold promotion involved a large expenditure of money which had to be paid in Rome. And the maintenance of the splendor of his court called for a liberal outlay, so that he was obliged to resort to extraordinary measures to replenish his coffers. He welcomed Pope Leo's plan of the disposal of indulgences, and gladly became his servant in its management ; for a division of the profits between Leo and Albert was a condition attached to the business agreement.

The first thing to be attended to now was to secure such subordinate officials as would understand how to carry on the traffic with indulgences in the most effective manner. And such were soon found. But the most zealous and vigorous among them all was without doubt the Dominican monk John Tetzel, born at Pirna in Saxony. His father was John Dietz, a goldsmith. As a child the son was called Dietzel, *i.e.*, little Dietz, from which arose the name Tetzel. He attended the University of Leipsic, and obtained the first degree in philosophy. Then he became a preaching friar. He had already served as preacher of indulgences, and had done a good business with the so-called papal "milk-and-butter letters." These were certificates granting permission, during the Lenten season, to partake of victuals prepared in part of butter and milk, though to do so was contrary to the laws of the Church. This former effective service

secured for him not only a new position as preacher and
seller of indulgences, but an appointment more honorable also, as Inquisitor, *i.e.*, as judge over all such as
presumed to deviate from the faith of the Church. And
he seems to have been well fitted by nature for his calling. He presented an imposing appearance and possessed a loud, strong voice. Exceedingly well did he
understand how to talk in a common way to the common
people. His ignorance he concealed by his audacity,
which never left him in the lurch. Nor did he refrain
from falsehood and exaggeration. And what he declared
concerning the effects of indulgences surpassed everything that had hitherto been said in their favor. In his
addresses to the people he maintained in plain speech :
" Christ has laid down His authority over all Christendom, until the day of judgment, and has intrusted the
Pope with plenary power in His stead. The Pope therefore can forgive each and every sin, whether already
committed or yet to be committed, and that without sorrow and repentance. The greatest guilt can be effaced
by purchasing a papal certificate of forgiveness. No
crime, however horrible and inconceivable in reality, is
excluded from this forgiveness. The indulgence cross
of the pope is not inferior in sacredness to the cross of
Christ, and hence the former must be honored as highly
as the latter." Even nature must be subject to the
power of these indulgences, said Tetzel. At Annaberg,
in Saxony, he declared that the hills surrounding the city
would be changed into solid silver if the people would
freely buy his indulgences. And whoever should presume to doubt the papal power to forgive sins, was
threatened with death at the stake, excommunication,
and eternal damnation.

The impression which his eloquence was calculated to

produce was further strengthened by the glorious display and the splendid festivities prepared to greet the advent of this preacher of indulgences. The region round about Magdeburg, Halberstadt, Zerbst, and Halle was traversed by Tetzel as if he were a distinguished prelate of the Church. He rode in a magnificent wagon surrounded by a mounted body-guard. He was met at the gates of every city he entered by the monks and other clergy, the municipal councillors, teachers and students, men and women, old and young, amid the ringing of bells, the singing of church choirs, and the burning of torches. At the head of the procession was carried the papal bull upon a velvet cushion and taken into the church. Here was erected a red cross, on which was fastened the papal banner. Then Tetzel mounted the pulpit and importuned the people with his admonitions and recommendations of indulgences : " Now, now is the day of grace come to your very doors ! Ye women, sell your veils and purchase indulgences with the proceeds !" He classified sins and misdemeanors, and fixed a definite tax for each and all. Thus, sacrilege or church robbery and perjury were rated at nine ducats ; * a murder already committed, at eight ducats ; adultery, at six ducats, etc. It is said that upon his treasure-chest was inscribed the motto :

> " Soon as the coin in the box doth ring,
> The soul can into heaven spring."

It was the Augustinian monk of Wittenberg who commanded this sinful traffic of the indulgence preacher to cease. Yet little did he dream how great a tempest he was conjuring up ! For the Pope himself, he entertained

---

* The silver ducat is about equal in value to the American dollar, and the gold ducat to about twice that amount.

the greatest reverence, and believed that he was at fault in but one thing, and that was this traffic in indulgences. In fact he persuaded himself to believe that the Pope knew nothing of the scandalous proceedings of Tetzel, and that, as soon as he should be informed of it, his righteous wrath would condemn the infamous traffic. Could he have known how greatly he was deceiving himself in this matter ?

Dr. Martin Luther, Master of the Liberal Arts and of Sacred Theology—thus he called himself in the superscription of his ninety-five theses. In these, however, for the first time, he publicly attacked the papal power, so far as it, according to his convictions, intrenched upon that domain which the Lord of Heaven and the Judge of earth had reserved unto himself.

 " When our Lord and Master Jesus Christ says : ' Repent,' etc., He wills that the believer's entire life shall be one of repentance." Thus begins the first thesis. And farther on he shows that God alone can forgive sins, since they are violations of His divine laws. The Pope has simply the right to pronounce and to declare the forgiveness which God grants. Every true Christian can partake, through God's grace, of all the gifts of Christ and His Church without any certificate of indulgence. Almsgiving and domestic economy are more meritorious than a lavish expenditure for indulgences. If the Pope knew how the Christians were being plundered by these indulgence preachers, he would rather see St. Peter's Church reduced to ashes than to have it erected with the flesh and blood of his sheep. The real treasure of the Church is the gospel of grace and of the glory of God. But, on the other hand, Dr. Luther would not suffer indulgence, as such, to be attacked. " He deserves punishment who resists the right of the Pope to declare the forgiveness of God and to remit ecclesiastical penances. And he that withstands the impudent audacity of the preachers of indulgences should be rewarded." " Blessed be he," says Luther, " who does this ;" " accursed be he who speaks against the truth of apostolic indulgences." And at the close he says : " Then away with all those prophets who cry to Christ's people, Peace, peace, when there is no peace ! A blessing upon those prophets who say to Christ's flock, The cross, the cross, though there be no cross ! Christians must be admonished to follow their Master, Christ, through pains, death, and hell ; and that they comfort themselves with the truth, that through much tribulation, rather than through assurance of peace, they must enter the kingdom of heaven !"

In a short time—in little more than two weeks—the theses of Dr. Martin Luther were read all over Germany. Numerous strangers who attended the anniversary festival of consecration at Wittenberg, in order that they might adore the many relics and other sacred treasures of the church, carried the news with them to their homes. Up to this time no one had been willing to bell the cat ! Great as was the discontent at the shameless proceedings of the traders in indulgences, equally great was the fear of opposing the Pope and the Church. But Luther said : " Whoever will begin anything good, let him see to it that he begin and venture it in reliance upon the favor of God, and never upon human comfort or assistance ; let him not fear any man, no, not the whole world !" Everywhere Luther's theses found prepared ground. Everywhere they were spoken of, and with anxious concern was he regarded who had ventured upon so bold a step ! Thus the name of the fearless Augustinian monk passed rapidly from nation to nation,

and many an inquiry was heard about the antecedents
and the experiences of the man, who had presumed to
take issue with the Pope and his adherents.   Let us also
review the days of his youth and follow the course of
his life, until he is called to teach in the university of the
Elector of Saxony, and there arises to protest against the
traffic in indulgences.

CHAPTER II.

"I AM a peasant's son; my father, grandfather, and great-grandfather were real peasants." Thus did Dr. Martin Luther express himself in a conversation with his friend Melanchthon. Whereupon the latter jokingly remarked, that Luther, had he remained in the home of his ancestors, might have been chosen chief magistrate of the village, or else have become head-servant over the rest!

The old paternal home was Möhra, also called More or Möre in the ancient chronicles. The village is located in the very centre of Germany. Proceeding southward about ten miles on the highway leading from Eisenach to Salzungen, Möhra is found, at some distance to the right of the main road, situated at the foot of a hill, one of the many mountain spurs which the Thuringian Forest projects into the valley of the river Werra. The ruler of that district is the Duke of Meiningen; in former days it was the Elector of Saxony. The village is a small and quiet place, cut off from the great highways of commerce, its most prominent building being the church, close to which is located the old Luther family mansion. The inhabitants of Möhra are a strong and sturdy people who derive a comfortable income from tilling the soil and raising cattle.*

---

* Three families by the name of Luther are still living in Möhra, engaged in the pursuit of farming.

And there it was that the father of Dr. Martin Luther, Hans Luder or Ludher, as the name was then written, resided with his wife, whose family name was Ziegler. But little is known concerning his ancestors. His grandfather was called Heine, which is the same as Henry. His grandmother died in the year 1521. Long before this Martin Luther's parents had removed from Möhra to Eisleben. Father Hans Luther, being a miner, was led to make the change by reason of his occupation. Copper ore had always been mined among the slate rock at Möhra, and to this day heaps of slate and slag are found by the roadside. But as mining may not have been very profitable there, Father Luther removed to Eisleben, a town that was then growing very rapidly. It is likely that the paternal inheritance did not afford a sufficient income for all the members of the family. Of two brothers information is at hand. One of them, Heinz Luther, was the owner of the farm and homestead.

An evil-minded, malicious report has of late years again been circulated, that Hans Luther was obliged to leave Möhra because he killed a peasant who had pastured his horses without permission on the meadows of the Luther farm. But there is no foundation whatever for such a story—even if the meadow is pointed out where the homicide is said to have occurred. The old inhabitants of Möhra knew nothing of this legend. Besides, it is difficult to see how Hans Luther could have saved himself from legal prosecution by his removal; for Eisleben was within easy reach—about seventy-five miles distant —and under the same princely jurisdiction.

At Eisleben Martin Luther was born. His mother knew the exact hour of his birth—between 11 and 12 ber ; yet she was not certain of the year. But the testimony of Jacob Luther, a brother of Martin, as well as the declaration of the latter, removes this uncertainty. For, according to both, Martin Luther was born in the year 1483. The house with the room in which he first saw the light of this world is still shown. It is located in the lower part of the city, near the church of St. Peter and St. Paul, in which Luther was baptized on the 11th of November, 1483, receiving the name of Martin because of the saint whose fame the day commemorated. In the year 1689 Eisleben was visited by a fearful conflagration, by which the Luther house was destroyed, save the lowest story, containing the room in which Martin was born.

After a short sojourn in Eisleben his parents removed to Mansfeld, but a few miles distant, also an important mining centre. The Earldom of Mansfeld embraced at one time a large extent of territory and was a land blessed from on high, so that an ancient chronicler says : "Whoever has a residence in this earldom is accounted happy." The little city is surrounded by hills, projecting spurs of the Hartz Mountains, and dominated by the battlements of the old castle of Mansfeld. The noble family has long since passed away ; the castle likewise has fallen into decay. Creeping ivy has woven a green net over its walls, and a luxurious growth of grass covers the courtyard. The prophecy of Dr. Martin Luther, when on a visit to the Counts of Mansfeld the wine flowed in streams, has been fulfilled : "My lords are fertilizing well ; grass will grow abundantly thereafter."

There, in yonder city, at the foot of the castle hill, Hans Luther established his home. And a hard struggle indeed it was for him, in the beginning, to provide for his family. "My father," thus narrates Dr. Martin Luther, "was a poor miner. My mother gathered wood and carried it home on her back, in order that her children might be educated. Both toiled slavishly for our sakes. In these days people would not do so." But after a little while they reached more comfortable circumstances. Hans Luther succeeded in purchasing a house on the main street of the city, whose oval portals surmounted by the Luther coat-of-arms, a rose and a crossbow, and the number 1530, bear testimony to this day. His numerous family—we read of six children besides Martin—may have continued to be a source of anxiety to Hans Luther. Yet, not only did he acquire a comfortable competency in his occupation (becoming the proprietor of two smelting furnaces), but he also gained the confidence of his fellow-citizens, who elected him a member of the town council.

The parents reared their son Martin in the fear of God and in the love of good works. But their discipline was strict and severe, as they themselves endured hard toil in gaining a livelihood. "My father," relates Luther, "on one occasion flogged me so severely that I ran away, and was embittered against him until he gradually regained my affections. On another occasion my mother, because of a mere nut, whipped me so hard that the blood flowed. Her severe and earnest treatment of me led me to enter a cloister and become a monk. But in their hearts they meant it well with me, and made but one mistake, in that they did not discern the different dispositions according to which all punishments should be administered. For we ought to punish so that the apple go hand in hand with the rod."

Thus was Martin Luther reared, so that he grew up to be bashful and humble-minded. And yet love was by no means wanting in his training. Often did he speak, in later years, of the sweet intercourse with his father, and with touching words did he refer to the benevolent love he enjoyed, even if his parents now and then went too far in their strict discipline. Indeed, the severity of the parental training sharpened his own conscience, so that he deeply felt his guilt before God, and never could he lightly pass over any sin or failing.

In Mansfeld he received his first instruction, being sent to school at a very early age. It is said that a good friend of the family many a time carried young Martin to and from the school, which was located in the upper part of the city. There he was instructed not only in reading and writing, but also in the rudiments of Latin. The discipline was so severe that Luther never forgot it. He tells of severe tortures with declensions and conjugations. "The schoolmasters in my days," says he, "were tyrants and executioners; the schools were jails and hells! And in spite of fear and misery, floggings and tremblings, nothing was learned. The young people were treated altogether too severely, so that they might well have been called martyrs. Time was wasted over many useless things, and thus many an able mind was ruined." He himself was innocently lashed fifteen times in the course of a single morning because he did not know what had not been taught him. On the other hand, he commends the use and preservation, thanks to God's might and providence, even under the Pope, of Common Prayer, the Psalter, the Lord's Prayer, the Creed and the Ten Commandments, also of many good hymns, both Latin and German. And although everything was in about the same disgraceful condition as in the days of Elijah, he nevertheless calls the Pope's church or house his "father-house," which he can never forget, because in it he was baptized and had learned the Catechism and the Holy Scriptures. He also praised the beautiful hymns which were sung in the papal church, but lamented that there were no preachers that could explain what they meant. Bitterly did he complain that, from childhood on, he had been so trained that he paled and trembled at the mere mention of the name of Christ, whom he had been taught to regard as a severe and angry judge.

His playmate and companion was Hans Reinecke, who afterward continued to reside, as citizen and overseer of the furnaces, in Mansfeld. Luther and Reinecke remained life-long friends. Together, at the age of fourteen, they went to Magdeburg, where there was a far-famed school. Thither Hans Luther sent his son Martin, because he wished him to become distinguished. Luther attended the instruction of the " Null-brothers." These " Null-brothers," or " Noll-brothers," were a pious brotherhood, banded together in a common life, to labor for the moral and religious welfare of the people, by means of sermons, instruction, and pastoral care. Luther remained but one year in Magdeburg. Why he left so soon is not known. But as his father could furnish little or nothing toward his support, he sent him to Eisenach, because in that city and neighborhood Luther had numerous relatives living who could assist him.

In the year 1498, a mere boy of the age of fifteen, he entered the city of Eisenach, where he was to remain four years. Here, at first, he had a very hard struggle to undergo. His relatives, one of whom was sexton of the church of St. Nicholas, were probably not in the position to assist him for any great length of time. He was therefore obliged, as a charity scholar, to appeal to the common sympathy of all men, as he had already done

in Magdeburg. In later years he himself says : " Do
not despise the boys that go from house to house asking
bread for the sake of God and singing the ' bread-
chorus.' I also was one of those ' bread-colts,' and
begged bread at the doors, especially in Eisenach, that
dear city." At another time he relates the following
incident : " It was at Christmas, and we were going
through the villages, from house to house, singing the
customary hymns about the Christ-child born at Bethle-
hem. It happened as we were singing before a farm-
house, at one end of the village, that the farmer
appeared, and, speaking in coarse, harsh language, inquired, ' Where are you boys ? ' At the same time he
carried with him several sausages, which he wished to
give us. But we were so badly frightened at his words
that we scattered and ran away, although we had no
good cause for so doing, especially since the farmer was
graciously inclined to present to us the sausages, and that
of his own good-will. But our hearts had grown timid
and fearful under the daily threatenings and tyrannizings
to which poor students were subjected by their teachers,
and hence our sudden fright. Meanwhile the farmer
hailed us again ; we dismissed our fears, returned, and
received the proffered gifts."

Thus Martin Luther was obliged to help himself since
his parents could not provide a complete support. But
good-fortune awaited him. For, because of his singing *
and heartfelt praying, he won the favor of Ursula Cotta,
who invited him to a seat at her table. She was of the
family of Schalbe, and the wife of Conrad Cotta, one of
the foremost citizens of the town. He was of noble
Italian descent, of a family that had grown wealthy

* Luther is said to have had a rich tenor voice.

through commerce. The Cotta family mansion was located in George Street, on the ground now occupied by the residence of Mr. Julius von Eichel.

In the Schalbean College, an institution under the control of the Franciscans, and which had been richly endowed by the family of Schalbe, Martin Luther received beneficiary aid, so that he could devote himself entirely to his studies during his four years' sojourn at Eisenach. The names of two of his teachers have been handed down to us : Wiegand, subsequently a pastor, who remained for many years in friendly correspondence with Luther; and John Trebonius, spoken of as a handsome and learned man and a poet. It is related of him, that whenever he entered the school-room he would take off his scholastic cap because, as he said, God had selected from among the students present many a magistrate, or chancellor, or learned doctor.

Luther, by reason of his superior perceptive faculties and of his natural eloquence, soon surpassed his fellow-students, and excelled them in linguistic exercises, as well in prose as in poetry.

At the close of the fifteenth century there existed in Eisenach three schools connected with the church of St. Nicholas, St. Mary's, and St. George's. The first-named was the oldest. The church of St. Nicholas, a Romanesque basilica, had received from Count Hermann, in the year 1208, a charter conferring the sole right and privilege of maintaining a school within the walls of the city. But this exclusive right does not seem to have been exercised for any great length of time. For besides St. Mary's, St. George's Church in the market-place established a school which surpassed the rest. Into this school Martin Luther was introduced in the year 1498. In the year 1544 this same institution was removed to the Dominican cloister, where it has been continued as the Latin School until this day.

After Martin Luther had diligently pursued his studies at Eisenach for four years, his parents sent him, at the age of eighteen, to the University of Erfurt, in the year 1501. This institution had acquired so great a name and reputation that all others, by way of contrast, were regarded as primary schools. With joyful assurance he passed out of the ancient gate of his beloved city, Eisenach, on the way to Erfurt, little dreaming that the castle (the Wartburg) which dismissed him with its farewell greeting would one day afford him a long-continued shelter.

In the meanwhile his parents had gained the means with which to furnish him a liberal support. "My dear father," relates Martin Luther, "in love and with fidelity, supported me at the University of Erfurt, and through his arduous labors I was enabled to go there." But Luther applied himself with equal toil and ardor to his task. Inspired by an eager desire for knowledge, he devoted himself with zeal and energy to his studies. His burning thirst for scholarly learning he could quench at the source of all the sciences. His most prominent teacher was Jodokus Trutvetter of Eisenach, a man of universal information and the chief support of the scholastic philosophy at Erfurt.

At the same time Erfurt was a principal seat and centre of that tendency in the scholastic world which sought to awaken the study of the ancient Greek and Latin classics. Luther likewise deeply interested himself in the same, especially in Ovid, Virgil, and Cicero. His object in reading them was to gain a variety of information, maxims of human wisdom, and a mirror of life. He diligently cultivated the acquaintance of his teachers and the circle of young men pursuing similar studies with himself. Among these he ranked as a learned philosopher and as an able musician. Especially did he cultivate music, learning how to sing and to play ·on the lute.

On St. Michael's day, in the year 1502, he received the degree of Bachelor of Philosophy, which was the lowest or first degree in philosophical honors. In two years he ·exchanged the modest dignity of a Bachelor for the higher eminence of a Master of Philosophy.* The talent of young Luther was admired by the entire university. It was now the wish of his father that he should become a jurist. With this object in view he began to attend lectures in the department of law. But suddenly the course of his life was turned into another direction.

* Equivalent to our modern degree of Doctor of Philosophy.

CHAPTER III.

On the 16th of July, 1505, Martin Luther invited his nearest friends to a farewell meeting. He did not intend to leave Erfurt, but rather to enter the Augustinian monastery located in that city. "To-day you see me, but no more hereafter," said he to his friends. These vainly endeavored to deter him from taking such a step. On the following day he knocked at the portals of the Augustinian cloister. His friends accompanied him, and weeping, bade him farewell. In a little while the gates of the monastery shut him off from the world. He became an Augustinian monk.

But since his parents had decided that he should become an advocate of the law, what led Luther to take a step that was not in accordance with their wishes? His father moreover was strenuously opposed to the entire system of monasticism. And why did Luther join the Augustinians?

His decision was suddenly made, and yet it had been long considered. His very disposition naturally impelled him to take this step. He treated the matter of an inner sanctification in a very serious manner, and could not content himself with outward services and ceremonies. The severe discipline of home training had sharpened his conscience. Again and again was he filled with the thoughts of becoming pious, and of fulfilling all the severe laws of God, in order that he might atone for the sins of his life, and reconcile God, the angry judge, to himself. He indulged in subtle inquiries upon religious questions of trifling import, was much concerned about his soul's salvation, and involved in numerous doubts. These occasioned him many a temptation. And yet he could not accuse himself of being guilty of any gross sins. Although he had been a jovial young fellow, he began his studies in the morning with a heartfelt prayer and by attending a church service. He also spent considerable of his time in the library of the university. Here, on one occasion, he found a Latin Bible, a book that he had never seen until his twentieth year. Greatly astonished, he noticed that there were many more texts, epistles and gospels, than he had read in the pericopes of the church or heard explained in the pulpit. And as he turned over the pages of the Old Testament his attention was arrested by the story of Samuel and Hannah, which he hurriedly read with great joy.

About this time he was greatly afflicted with bodily ailments. A long and serious illness confined him to his bed. Thoughts of death troubled him. But one of his student friends comforted him, saying, "My friend, be of good cheer; you will not die of this sickness. God will yet make a great man of you, who will comfort many people."

Not long after this a dangerous accident befell him. He was on his way home to visit his parents at Eastertide. But a few miles distant from Erfurt, the sword which he carried, student-fashion, accidentally wounded him in the leg, injuring an artery. While his companion hastened to procure a surgeon, Luther, lying upon his back, quenched the flow of blood. But the leg began to swell, and overcome by the fear of death, he cried out, "Help me, O Virgin Mary!" And when at night the wound again began to flow and he grew faint, he prayed once more to the Virgin Mary. Had he died it would have been in the hope of St. Mary.

A short time after this experience he was again greatly disturbed by the death of a friend, who was either murdered or otherwise suddenly removed from this earth. Luther mightily felt, as never before, the pangs of conscience that had often troubled him. A deep melancholy overcame him. Mournfully the youthful scholar wandered about.

In addition to all this, another circumstance happened which hastened his decision to seek his soul's salvation in the monastic holiness recommended by the church. He had been on a visit to his parents. On his return to the university he had reached the village of Stotternheim, near Erfurt, when a furious thunderstorm burst over him, and he fell frightened to the earth, crying out, "Deliver me, St. Ann,* and I will become a monk." Though he regretted having made this vow, he felt himself bound to keep it. And this impelled him to monkhood, for, as he said himself, he never could find comfort in his Christian baptism, and was always much concerned to obtain the favor of God through his own piety.

And thus, in the year 1505, he entered the monastery of the Augustinians,† an order which in Erfurt and else-

---

* St. Ann was the patron saint of the miners, and hence revered by all in that section of country.

† The Augustinians, or Hermits of St. Augustine, trace their origin to Augustine, the Bishop of Hippo, who lived 354–430 A.D. In England they are called Black Friars from the color of their habit. In Philadelphia they have a convent with church, and at Villanova, about fifteen miles from the city, a college with monastery.

where was highly respected. Its monks were free from the corruptions of monastic life, from idleness, hypocrisy, and other evils. They were, on the other hand, very active in preaching and in exercising pastoral care, and zealously cultivated the study of theology.

For two days Luther's friends besieged the gates of the monastery in hope that he would return to them again. But he came not. He wrote to his parents informing them of his entrance into the Augustinian cloister, and asking for their approval of his action. This the father would not give. Luther informs us of the impression which the letter made upon his parents : ".My father well-nigh went mad over it, was badly displeased and would not give his consent. He wrote to me in a very plain and direct manner—whereas before this he had always addressed me very courteously—and withheld from me his favor."

About that time Father Luther lost two of his sons by the plague. His friends entreated him to sacrifice unto God his dearest treasure by permitting his remaining son to enter into the divinely sanctified order of the ministry. At last the father was persuaded to give his consent, saying, "Let it be done ; God grant that the project may succeed." But he consented with an unwilling mind, a sorrowful will, and an unhappy heart, because he would rather have seen his son become a jurist, an advocate of the law.

In the monastery every one was proud to see the youthful and learned scholar in the garb of the order, the black cowl with the scapulary. Yet the new arrival could not be exempted from any of the most menial services which it was customary to impose upon the novices in order to break their self-will and to overcome their pride. Thus Luther was obliged to assist in the cleaning of the cells.

He was also sent out with the beggar's sack, through the streets of the city, to solicit food and money. And although he himself did not feel humiliated in the performance of these menial duties—for he was inspired with a burning desire faithfully to fulfil his vows of poverty and obedience—yet the professors of the university interposed their objections. Since he had been a member of the university, they petitioned the prior of the cloister that Luther might be excused from performing such unclean and humiliating labors. The vicar of the order, John von Staupitz,* also interposed on his behalf, and requested that he be more gently treated, and that he have time for study. And when an order was issued enjoining upon all Augustinian monks diligent reading, reverent hearing, and zealous learning of the Holy Scriptures as a sacred duty, Luther entered upon their study with extraordinary zeal. He read the Bible completely so many times that he could turn immediately to any desired passage, to the great astonishment of his noble patron, John von Staupitz.

At the expiration of a year, his novitiate being ended, he was solemnly received into the order, and in 1507 he was ordained a priest. At this latter service he again met his father, whom he had not seen since his entrance into the monastery. Father Luther had accepted the invitation of his son Martin, and was present at the festivities

* Johann von Staupitz was born at Meissen, and died in Salzburg, December 28th, 1524. He was instrumental in establishing the University of Wittenberg, and became the first Dean of its theological faculty. He was the intimate friend and supporter of Luther until the latter finally broke with the papacy, when Staupitz retired to Salzburg in the year 1519. Here he changed his order and became Abbot of the Benedictine monastery of St. Peter, in which position he died in 1524.

with a stately array of friends and relatives. Whilst at table, the young priest turned the conversation upon his entrance into the monastery, and thus addressed his father: "My dear Father, why were you so angry at and so bitterly opposed to my becoming a monk, and perhaps even now are not pleased with it? Is it not a very peaceful and divine occupation?" Father Luther then arose, and, not having changed his opinion upon the act of his son, addressed himself to the learned doctors, masters, and all others present, saying: "Ye learned gentlemen, have ye not read in the Holy Scripture the command, Honor your father and your mother"? And when Martin answered, supported by others, that he had been called from heaven amidst fearful manifestations, Father Luther replied: "Would to God that it be not a deception and a spook of the devil!" From this it appears that he had given his consent, but very unwillingly. And then he added: "I am indeed obliged to be here, both to eat and to drink, but I had rather be elsewhere."

The new office brought to the young priest new cares and new anxieties. For very seriously did he regard his vow to dedicate himself and his life unto God. "True it is," says he, "that I was a pious monk, and so strictly did I keep the vows of my order that I may say if ever a monk has entered heaven through monkery, then I also could have entered. All my fellow-monks who knew me will confirm this statement. And if I had continued much longer, I would have tortured myself to death with vigils and prayers, reading, and other work. If ever there was a man who, before the gospel was made known unto him, highly esteemed the teachings of the Fathers and the decrees of the Popes, and with great earnestness contended for the same, then it was I who did so in a peculiar manner. And with a hearty zeal did I maintain and defend them, as if they had been so much of pure holiness, and especially necessary for the soul's salvation.   And I exerted myself to the utmost to obey such precepts, and to punish and castigate my body with fasts and vigils, prayers and other exercises, more than all those who are my bitterest enemies and persecutors.   Hence, I now teach that such fool-works can never justify any one in the sight of God.   And so diligently did I practise such buffoonery that I fell into superstition, and imposed more upon my body than it could bear without injury to health.   I heartily and earnestly adored the Pope, not for the sake of rich benefices, church endowments, and eminent preferments ; but what I did that I.did in truth, out of a pure and simple heart, and with a right earnest zeal, because I thought it was doing good, and that it would redound to the honor of God."

And yet, no matter how much he studied and prayed, no matter how severely he castigated himself with fasting and watching, he found no peace to his soul.   Even when he imagined that he had satisfied the law, he often despaired of getting rid of his sins and of securing the grace of God.   In the hymn, " Now rejoice ye Christian people," * we learn the condition of his heart.

Often did he engage in violent soul-conflicts.   But the quiet seclusion of the cloister and his zealous study of the Holy Scriptures combined to further his spiritual development so rapidly, that the turning-point of his soul-conflicts was reached before he left the monastery. More than by any one else was he assisted in this by the noble Vicar-General of the Augustinian Cloisters, John

* In German : " Nun freut euch, lieben Christen gemein."
This hymn is said to have been the means of converting hundreds
to the cause of the Reformation.

von Staupitz, who had also made a special study of the
Scriptures to the guidance of his inner life.   To him
Luther opened his heart, and unto him he revealed his
doubts and anxieties about religious matters.   On one
occasion, when they were conversing about repentance,
Staupitz said, "There is no true repentance other than
that which flows from the love of God and His righteousness."   This word penetrated Luther's soul as the
sharpened arrow of the warrior.   He searched in the
Scriptures and found to his sweet joy that all the words
of the Bible agreed with the above statement ; so that,
whereas formerly there was no word in Scripture more
bitter to him than repentance, there was now no other
word that was sweeter and that sounded more agreeable.

An old brother monk also made a deep impression
upon Luther with his words.   When Luther bewailed
his temptations, the old monk referred him to the passage in the Apostles' Creed which says, " I believe in the
forgiveness of sins."   And furthermore, to a declaration
of St. Bernard the preacher :   " But also believe that
through Christ thy sins are forgiven thee.   That is the
testimony of the Holy Spirit in thy heart when he says,
' Thy sins are forgiven thee.'   For it is the apostle's
teaching that man through grace is justified by faith."

Day and night, says Luther, the sense and the connection of this apostolic word occupied his mind.   Finally an all-merciful God granted him to see that Paul
and the Gospel proclaim a righteousness which is bestowed
upon us through God's grace.   For God forgives the
sins of those who believe in His word of grace, justifies
them, and presents them with eternal life.   With this the
gates of paradise were opened to him, and thenceforth the
whole import of the divine word of salvation was clearly
revealed.

This knowledge was the glorious fruit of his sojourn in the monastery at Erfurt. Besides a valuable fund of information which he there acquired, he was led to independent research and personal investigation. And thus it came to pass that John von Staupitz recommended Martin Luther, at the age of twenty-five, to a professorship in the newly founded University of Wittenberg.

CHAPTER IV.

THE University of Wittenberg was founded in the year 1502 by the Elector of Saxony, Duke Frederick the Wise.* A faithful care of his subjects, sincere love of science, and a deep piety combined to ripen in him the resolve to establish a university for his people. And first of all he was concerned to procure eminent teachers for his new institution. In this he made use of the counsel of John von Staupitz. The latter immediately remembered the distinguished Augustinian monk in the cloister of Erfurt, and recommended him to the Elector as a young man of excellent disposition and of comprehensive attainments. The Elector approved of the choice, and called Martin Luther to Wittenberg in 1508.

His departure from Erfurt was taken so suddenly that his nearest friends were scarcely informed of it. The city of Wittenberg, in contrast with Erfurt, made a poor impression upon him. It numbered but 3000 inhabitants,

---

* Frederick III., surnamed the Wise, was born in Torgau, January 17th, 1463 ; died at Lochau, May 5th, 1525. After the death of the Emperor Maximilian I. he declined the crown of Germany, which, by his advice, was conferred upon Charles V. For this act he has been variously judged by historical writers. On his death-bed he received the Lord's Supper with both bread and wine, and thus sealed his adherence to the cause of the Reformation.

was badly built, and not in a flourishing condition.   At
the university Luther began by teaching the philosophical
sciences.   This was not altogether agreeable to him.   He
would gladly have exchanged philosophy for theology,
especially for that theology which penetrates to the ker-
nel of the nut, the flower of the wheat, and the marrow
of the bones.   He at once made the necessary preparations for obtaining the several theological degrees, in order
that he might soon obtain his aim.   The first degree,
Bachelor of Theology, he received in 1509.   He now
began to contend against the fundamental principle of
casuistry, and to search for the true and certain ground of
our salvation.   The writings of the prophets and apostles,
which have proceeded from the mouth of God, he regarded as higher, surer, and profounder than all sophis-
try and scholastic theology—at which well-informed men
were surprised !   Thus one of them often remarked :
" This monk is leading all the learned doctors astray ; he
is bringing forth new doctrines, and is going to reform the
whole Roman Church."

But scarcely had he begun to teach in his new position
when he was called back to Erfurt, for what reason is not
known.   When after a short absence he had returned
to Wittenberg, he received instructions from his order to
proceed to Rome.   His mission was to secure the settle-
ment of a dispute that had arisen within the Augustinian
order.   This was an evidence of the confidence reposed
in the youthful monk.

And so Luther proceeded to the Eternal City, the seat
of the head of the Church.   As a reverent pilgrim he arrived at Rome, after a six weeks' journey.   Seeing the
city from afar he fell upon the earth and cried out,
" Hail ! thou sacred Rome !"   And yet he found many
things different from what he had expected.   His expe-

rience there made a lasting impression upon him. "I would not have taken one hundred thousand florins not to have seen Rome. Among other coarse talk, I heard one reading mass, and when he came to the words of consecration, he said, ' Thou art bread and shalt remain bread, thou art wine and shalt remain wine.' What was I to think of this? And, moreover, I was disgusted at the manner in which they could 'rattle off' a mass as if it had been a piece of jugglery, for long before I reached the Gospel lesson, my neighbor had finished his mass and cried out to me, 'Enough! enough! hurry up and come away,' etc. !"

Filled with awe and reverence, he had come to Rome, and had hoped to find peace for his soul. " I was one of those frantic saints in Rome ; I ran about all the churches and crypts, and believed all their shameless, impudent lies. I also read mass, perhaps ten times, and I very much regretted that my father and mother were still alive, for I should have been delighted to deliver them from purgatory with my masses, and with other precious works and many prayers." On his knees he crept up Pilate's staircase, the *Scala Sancta* or holy stairway, which was said to have been brought from the judgment hall to Rome and placed in the chapel of St. John's Church of the Lateran. Luther did this in order to receive indulgence. And yet he felt, in doing such a work, as if a voice in thunder tones were crying out to him : " The just shall live by faith" (Rom. 1 : 17).

And yet, in spite of all the repulsive things Luther saw in Rome, he did not lose his faith in the Papacy. Later in life he used his experience in that city as a sharp sword. The shameful cruelties and the immoral life of the last Pope, Alexander, were still held in lively remembrance. Concerning Julius II. he heard and saw nothing but what was worldly. He writes as follows "Rome is now making a grand display. The Pope i: riding about in triumph, drawn by stallions, and the Sacra ment (*i.e.* the host or consecrated wafer) is carried aroun(with him upon a beautiful white stallion !" Julius II had already begun the erection of St. Peter's Church Luther little thought at the time, that in a few year that very building should lead to the outward provocatior for protesting against the abuses of the Papacy. Hi: national pride was often wounded in Rome by hearing his fellow-countrymen contemptuously spoken of as th(" stupid Germans," or as the " German beasts." After : month's residence in the cloister of " S. Maria del Popo lo," on the " Piazza del Popolo," Luther set out on hi: return home. He had not tarried longer than was neces sary ; for, said he, " Whoever goes to Rome for the firs time is looking for a rogue ; whoever goes again will fin(him ; and whoever goes the third time will return witl him." *

After Luther had returned to Wittenberg he applie(himself most zealously to the study of the Holy Scrip tures. At the urgent recommendation of Dr. Staupitz h(applied for and received the degree of Doctor of Sacre(Theology. "I was called and compelled to take th(doctorate, without thanks and out of pure obedience I was obliged to assume the labor, and to vow and promis(to teach the most precious Holy Scriptures sincerely an(honestly"—thus writes Martin Luther.

Inasmuch as the scholastic theology then current neg lected the study of the Bible, Luther directed his whol(attention to the latter. He began with lectures upor

---

* During his short stay in Rome, Luther, always eager to learn took lessons in Hebrew from a noted rabbi, Elias Levita.

the Psalms, and he explained them in such a way that, in
the opinion of Melanchthon, a new light of doctrine
arose after a long dark night. In Luther's explanations
he showed the difference between Law and Gospel. He
confronted the error that men could merit the forgiveness
of their sins through their own works, or that they could
be justified before God through outward observances, as
the Pharisees had taught. To substantiate this he appealed to his own researches in the Scriptures, to the
epistles of the Apostle Paul, and to the writings of St.
Augustine, the great master of his order. His interpretation of the Psalms was followed by lectures upon the
Epistles to the Romans and Galatians. And while at
work upon these sacred books, that fundamental truth,
which he subsequently defined as the article of a standing
or a falling church, became firmly rooted in his heart and
mind.

But he did not anticipate that the question how sinful
man can prevail before God and secure salvation would
ever lead to a controversy between him and the Church.
More and more this truth developed into a certainty, that
a gracious God justified the believers by placing them in
their rightful relations to Him, and by inwardly trans-
forming them. It is faith in the heart of man which
carries with it a decisive significance for communion with
God. Faith is the central point, the marrow, the direct
path on which the grace of God through our Saviour
Jesus Christ can be secured. With this faith, and because of this Saviour, we prevail before God, we possess
the certainty of sonship and salvation. Luther views the
law as the substance of God's holy demands with reference to man's will and works, which demands the sinner
cannot fulfill. He regards the Gospel as the joyful message and presentation of that forgiving grace of God

which must be received by a simple faith, By the law, says Luther, sinners are judged, condemned, and executed. He too had to perspire and agonize under its power as in the hand of a taskmaster and hangman. The Gospel lifts up those that are bowed down, and makes them alive through faith begotten in the heart by the joyful message. God works in both : in the former, the law, which is really foreign to him as a God of love ; and in the latter, the gospel, his own peculiar work of love, for which, however, he must first prepare the sinner through the law.

But the more profoundly he studied the Scriptures, the more positively did he turn away from Aristotle, whose philosophy for a long time had prevailed in the Church. In this he ran counter to the controlling teachings of the scholastic theologians as well as of his former instructors.

Hence the University of Wittenberg was subjected to many a condemnatory criticism. But this did not disconcert Luther ; on the contrary, his views were strengthened by reading the sermons of the pious theologian Tauler.* Over against a formal ecclesiasticism he found in the writings of the latter the profoundest religious convictions of a Christian mind. The strivings of Luther's soul for intimate communion with God awakened a loud echo in the writings of this pious man. Such depth and inwardness of soul were peculiar to Luther. His first publication was a tract, entitled " German Theology," which he issued in 1516 and again in 1518. His

---

* John Tauler, a German mystic, was born in Strasburg in 1290, and died there in 1361. He was one of the so-called " friends of God," an unorganized fraternity of mystic thinkers among the clergy and laity. In his teachings he insisted upon heart and soul worship, and freely denounced ecclesiastical abuses.

first original work was a translation of and commentary upon the seven penitential Psalms (6th, 31st, 50th, 101st, 129th, 142d), which appeared in 1517.

The influence of Tauler upon Luther appears also in the sermons of the latter. He zealously contended against those who prided themselves upon their meritorious works and their self-conceived holiness ; he warned against the presumption of self-righteousness as against a most dangerous snare, and pointed out the way upon which the soul, by simple faith in the proffered word of grace, would be led to its God and Saviour. At the same time he declaimed against the practical 'abuses and errors of the ecclesiastical religious life, and expressed himself boldly against the lives of monks and priests, and against the absurdity of saints' legends. But the divine origin and the divine right of the hierarchical offices of the Papacy, the episcopacy, and of the priesthood, and the infallibility of the Church thus governed, remained to him inviolable. In his sermons, at this time, he still prayed to the Virgin Mary. He regarded the Bohemians, who had separated from the Church, as sinful heretics.

And yet the turning-point in his career had come. The scandalous proceedings of the traffic in indulgences forced him into the arena of battle. And the first step once having been taken, he could not retreat. For then he must defend and maintain that which he had experienced in severe conflicts of the soul and proclaimed in public sermons.

He now advanced beyond the narrow circle. With the rapidity of the lightning's flash his name was carried through all Germany, and the hearts of those who were in earnest about their soul's salvation, about their faith and their inner purification, of those to whom the indulgences and other abuses of the Church were a scandal and a shame, beat in unison with his own.

The Church accepted the challenge and entered into conflict. At first it was believed that the Monk of Wittenberg would soon be crushed, as others had been before him. Yet he proved himself to be a match for the Pope and the Church. Luther's own opinion upon his first step we have in his own words: " I have permitted my 'dispositions and propositions,' which I set up in the beginning of my conflict against indulgences, to see the light of day, especially because the importance and the successful progress of the cause, which in the providence of God may follow, shall not exalt me or render me proud. For through these same theses I publicly proclaimed my shame—that is, the great weakness and ignorance which overcame me in the beginning with great fear and trembling. Heedless and alone I entered upon this conflict, and because I could not retreat, I not only conceded much to the Pope in many and important articles, but I also willingly and earnestly revered him. For I was a miserable, despised brother, who at that time resembled a corpse more than a human being. In this condition did I confront the majesty of the Pope, in whose very presence the kings of this world, yea the whole earth, stood abashed, and in accordance with whose will all was done. What my heart endured and suffered during the first two years, and by what genuine humility, I might almost say despair, I was possessed—of this experience little is known by those certain spirits who afterward attacked the majesty of the Pope with great pride and boldness. But I, who stood alone in the conflict, was not so happy, confident, and sure of the result. For I was in ignorance then of much that I now know, thanks be to God ! I disputed, and was eager to be taught. And since the dead and the dumb masters—that is, the books of the theologians and jurists—could not satisfactorily inform me, I demanded counsel of the living and desired to hear the Church of God. There I found many pious men that were pleased with my theses and highly esteemed them. But it was impossible for me to regard and acknowledge them as living members of the Church, endowed with the Holy Spirit, but simply as Pope, cardinals, bishops, theologians, jurists, monks, and priests. Hence I awaited the Spirit's coming, for I had eagerly accepted their teaching, so that I was benumbed and did not know whether I was awake or asleep. And when I had overcome, by the Scriptures, all the arguments that were in the way, it was with great fear, trouble, and labor that I, by the grace of Christ, finally overcame this last argument, viz., that one ought to hear the Church. For with much greater earnestness, with genuine reverence, and with my whole heart, did I regard the Pope's church as the true Church far more than do these shameful and blasphemous perverters who now so highly exalt the Pope's church."

Soon after this he sent his theses, and a further explanation of the same, to the Bishop of Brandenburg, and through Staupitz to the Pope. To Staupitz he wrote : " Moreover, to my enemies I have but this to say, in the words of Reuchlin : * ' Whoever is poor fears nothing, for he can lose nothing.' Possessions I have none ; fame and honor, if I have ever enjoyed them, are only lost by him who has long since begun to lose them. But one

* John Reuchlin was born in Pforzheim in 1455, and died in Stuttgart in 1522. He was one of the foremost advocates of the study of classical literature, and especially of Greek and Hebrew. He is said to have published the first Hebrew work printed in Germany. He secretly favored Protestantism, but never publicly renounced his connection with the Roman Catholic Church.

thing remains : my frail body weakened by constant
troubles. If with craft or force they deprive me of that,
thinking that they are doing God a service, they may perhaps make me poorer by an hour or two of my life.
But I am content in having my dear Redeemer and Mediator, my Lord Jesus Christ. I will sing unto Him as long
as I live.

Concerning his theses Luther said, some he would
prove ; the rest he would discuss, and desire further information. Powerfully and emphatically he continued
to teach the evangelical doctrine of repentance and faith.
He denied to the saints the possession of any superfluous
merit which might be of benefit to us idle and indolent
sinners. But, on the other hand, he clung to a belief in
purgatory, and cared not what heretics might babble
against it. He had a good opinion of the reigning Pope,
and hoped that he would become his patron in the conflict against the bold-faced traders in indulgences. But
Rome itself he declared to be the true Babylon. For the
sake of God's order and appointment, it was necessary
to yield in all things with reference to the authority of
the Pope, even to respect his unrighteous judgments,
yet without approving them, but simply because of the
general command against self-help.

But to the contrary he speaks in another passage : " I
do not care whether the Pope is pleased or displeased :
he is but a man like other men. I hear and obey the
Pope as pope—that is, when he speaks in harmony with
the laws of the Church, and when he governs himself accordingly, or when he proclaims the decisions of a Church
council—but never when he simply utters his own individual opinions. The Pope alone can create no new articles of faith, but can merely give his opinion in accordance with those that have been established, and also

decide questions at issue concerning the faith.'' But in
no event did Luther wish to remain at variance with the
Church and the Pope. '' Accept or reject, grant life or
death, as it pleaseth thee''—thus did he subject himself
to the authority of the Pope. Deeply he bewailed the sad
condition of the Church. '' The Church,'' said he, '' needs
a reformation ; but this should not be the work of one
man,· like the Pope ; nor of many cardinals, as it was in
the last general Church Council ; but of the whole world,
or rather of God alone. The time of this reformation is
known only to Him who has created time.''

Many regarded the appearance of Luther as the advent
of this time. Thus a monk of Steinlausig, when he had
read the theses, cried out with joy, '' He is the one that
will do it ; he has come for whom we have so long
waited.'' And others said, '' Now has the time arrived
when the darkness must be expelled out of Church and
school, and the pure doctrine return to the churches.''
And old Reuchlin remarked, '' Thank God they have
now found a man that will give them so much of hard
work to do that they will suffer me, poor old man that I
am, to depart in peace.''

Others were not so confident. '' Go to your cell and
pray, my brother, that the Lord will have mercy upon
you''—thus said many a one that thought so vast an
undertaking by an insignificant monk against the Pope—
of whose might and influence kings were afraid—would
surely come to grief. '' My dear Brother Martin,'' said
an aged Westphalian clergyman, '' if you can do away
with purgatory and the traffic in indulgences, you are
indeed a great man !''

Luther's prior and sub-prior came and entreated him
not to bring reproach upon his order, for the other orders
were already leaping with joy, saying that they were not

the only ones guilty of offenses, but that now the Augustinians were also in the fire and bearers of shame. Luther replied to them, " Dear fathers, if this work has not been begun in God's name, it will soon come to naught; but if it has been begun in His name, then let Him rule as He will !"

The University of Wittenberg took his part. His system of theology was the prevailing one ; his lectures drew crowds of hearers.

The Elector of Saxony left the matter in the hands of God, attentively followed its progress, and neither praised nor blamed. What he recognized as good and true he was not disposed to assist in suppressing. The Emperor Maximilian, who had read Luther's theses, sent a message to the Elector requesting him to take good care of the monk, for it might yet come to pass that his services would be needed. " His theses are not to be despised," said he ; " he will make it very lively for the priests."

But above all others did the preachers and traders in indulgences thunder against Luther, threatening that in less than a fortnight he would be burned at the stake. His enemies, foremost among them the mountebank Tetzel, sought to annihilate him with counter-theses. But they failed in their efforts, for Luther quieted them in a very forcible and expeditious manner. Others remarked, that if he had received a good bishopric he would highly exalt indulgences instead of rejecting them.

Luther replied, in turn, that if he had had a bishopric in view he would not have spoken as he did ; for they ought not to suppose him to be ignorant of the manner in which bishoprics were obtained in Rome. He was now charged with irreverence against the Pope. This he repelled by saying, " The Pope is a human being who

may be deceived, especially by cunning and hypocritical
people. But God is the truth, and cannot be deceived.
Hence I entreat my enemies not to frighten me hereafter
by flattering the Pope, nor by their renowned teachers ;
but that they instruct and conquer me by well-grounded
declarations of the Bible and of the Pope, if they are
indeed bent upon carrying off the victory at all haz-
ards.''

But how did the Pope act in this violent conflict ? Two
of his utterances are recorded : "Brother Martin is a very
ingenious fellow ; but the conflict itself is merely a quarrel between jealous monks.'' And again : "A drunken
German must have written these theses ; as soon as he
becomes sober he will change his mind.'' The highest
circles of Rome, and the immediate attendants upon the
Pope were guilty of the same depreciative and contempt-
uous treatment of the Germans and of Luther's theses.
In their replies the "obscure German" and his "dog-
biting" theses were treated in the most derogatory manner. They viewed the Pope as the Church of Rome, and
the Roman Church as equivalent to the universal Christian Church. But whoever presumed to question the
right of the Church to do anything it pleased, was a
heretic.

Thus were they disposed in Rome, at least in the beginning, to assume the position of a haughty security. It
was purposed, in a short time, by means of the papal
power, to put an end to this unruly German monk. A
court of inquisition was appointed, and Luther was cited
to appear before it on the 7th of August—within 60
days he was expected to report himself personally in
Rome.

But before this time had expired the Pope took up
other measures against Luther. The tremendous ex-

citement which the 95 theses had caused no doubt impelled him to more vigorous proceedings. Hence the Pope wrote to the Elector and entreated him to avoid the very appearance of the guilt of complicity, and to deliver Luther, the child of wickedness, into the hands of his legate, before whom he was to vindicate himself. But secretly the Elector was ordered to secure the arrest of the heretic with all the means in his power. His adherents were also to be arrested, and an interdict laid upon every place where Luther was tolerated.

But the movement was not to be so quickly and so easily suppressed as the Pope imagined. He was obliged to take into account the influential tendencies prevailing in the German Empire at that time. And these were not favorable to him ; for everywhere grievous charges were preferred, and bitter complaints were heard concerning the violent and unlawful proceedings of the Pope, and especially in reference to the immense sum of money that was annually carried to Rome. Accordingly, when in the year 1518 the Pope again desired the grant of a large imperial tax, ostensibly for a war against the Turks, an embittered feeling was manifested, and it was publicly charged that the genuine Turks were to be found in Italy ! The Imperial Parliament declined to accede to his request, but drew up a long list of grievances against the Pope : as touching the large sums of money which he collected from German benefices, and which, under various pretexts, he extorted ; as to the unlawful assumption of power in making ecclesiastical appointments in Germany ; as to a continued violation of the ratified concordats, etc.

Luther profited by all this without being aware of it. But the Pope was obliged to take these circumstances into account, and therefore to treat him with consideration.

Thus, the papal legate Cajetan* was very careful not to increase the universal feeling of excitement in his proceedings against Luther. Indeed he promised the Elector of Saxony to hear him in Augsburg, and to treat him with fatherly kindness. And thus Luther, in accordance with the desire of the university authorities, and agreeably to his own wishes, was cited to appear in Augsburg.

---

* Cajetan or Cajetanus (Italian : Gaëtano) was so called from his birthplace, Gaëta, in Italy. His real name was Jacob de Vio, but he afterward substituted Thomas for Jacob, in honor of Thomas Aquinas, his scholastic master. Cajetan was a zealous Dominican, and became general of his order. He was an able scholar, a very skilful intriguer, a haughty diplomatist, and withal one of the most prominent figures in the history of the Reformation. He was born in 1469, and died in Rome in 1534.

CHAPTER V.

In September, 1518, Luther set out on his journey. On the 28th he arrived at Weimar, and lodged in the monastery. On the following day he preached in the castle church in the presence of the Elector, who at that time had established his court in Weimar. Basing his discourse upon the text, Matthew 18 : 1, etc., he warned against a proud self-righteousness and sanctimoniousness, and against the accompanying vices of envy and avarice. In so doing he expressly castigated the bishops, who ought to appear in the form of servants, but who, like Antichrist, seated themselves in the temple of God, and used the imparted powers of their office simply to their own advantage.

He did not refer, however, to his own position. " My thoughts," said he afterward, " on the journey were these : Now I must die ; and often did I remark, What a reproach will I be to my parents !" He undertook the journey on foot, in company with a young monk of Wittenberg, by way of Nuremberg. Here his friend Link* met him. When in the neighborhood of Augsburg Luther was overcome by bodily weakness. Faint-hearted friends had often warned him on the way not to enter

* Link was the successor of Staupitz as Vicar-General of the Augustinian order, and the Reformer of the Province of Altenburg.

Augsburg. But in reply to them he said, "In Augsburg, even in the midst of mine enemies, Jesus Christ also reigns. May Christ live, even if Martin should die." Arriving in the neighborhood of Augsburg, he informs us that he became very uncomfortable, that a demon tortured him with evil thoughts. On the 7th of October he arrived in Augsburg, where he was hospitably entertained, at first in the Augustinian and then in the Carmelite monastery. He was already the subject of conversation everywhere in the city. Everybody, said he, wished to see this Herostratus * who had kindled so great a conflagration.

Luther immediately announced his arrival to the papal legate. But he did not venture to meet the latter until his friends, to whom the Elector had recommended him, had obtained a safe-conduct from the Emperor, who was then on a hunt in that neighborhood ; for the Italians are not to be trusted, said Luther. In the meanwhile a servant of the Cardinal Legate delivered the following message to him : "The Cardinal offers you his sincere favor ; why do you fear ? He is a very affable father."

An Italian, a friend of Cajetan, also called upon Luther, sent, according to common belief, by the Cardinal himself. Like a genuine Italian, said Luther, this one regards the whole matter in a very light-hearted manner, as if it turned about these six letters : *revoca* (*i.e.* recant). Then the Italian added, laughingly :

"Do you really think the Elector Frederick would go to war on your account ?"

To which Luther replied :

* An Ephesian, who on the night in which Alexander the Great was born, in 356 B.C., set fire to the magnificent temple of Diana, at Ephesus, which was completely destroyed. His self-confessed motive was to render his name immortal.

" That I would not desire."

" And where, then, will you remain ?" returned the former.

" Under the heavens," said the latter.

" But what would you do were the Pope and cardinals to have you in their power ?" continued the Italian.

" I would show them all honor and reverence," concluded Luther.

Whereupon the former departed laughing, and with a gesture of contempt. But Luther's resolve stood fast ; rather would he die than to recall what he had taught and written. The idea of appealing to a council, in case of necessity, also occurred to him, and was developing in his mind.

After the letter of safe-conduct had arrived, Luther proceeded to the papal legate. His friends had directed him as to the proper manner of meeting a cardinal and a papal legate. Luther prostrated himself in the presence of the Cardinal, and even after he had been told to arise he remained in a kneeling position until he was again commanded. And since neither the Cardinal nor any one else ventured to speak, Luther believed that this silence was an intimation that he should begin. Accordingly he delivered himself of the following : " Reverend Father, in obedience to the citation of his Papal Holiness, and to the demand of my gracious Lord, the Elector of Saxony, 1 have appeared and confess that I published the 95 Theses. And I am in obedience both ready and willing to hear what accusations have been brought against me, and if I have erred, to be informed and corrected." The legate then addressed him in a gracious and fatherly manner, and in the name of the Pope plainly demanded of him that he recant his errors and promise to abstain thereafter from the promulgation of all views that might distract the Church. Two articles he should recall and withdraw : first, the denial that the "indulgence-treasure" of the Church is the merit of our Lord Jesus Christ ; secondly, his maintenance that a person who wishes to receive the Lord's Supper must above all things possess the faith and the inner conviction that his sins will be forgiven him. Hereupon a discussion ensued between Luther and Cajetan. The attendants of the latter audibly tittered when they heard the explanations of the Augustinian monk, so strange and curious did they seem to the Italians. In vain did Luther appeal to the Bible and its declarations concerning faith. The Cardinal then confronted Luther with the papal authority, which was above that of councils, the Church and the Scriptures, and declared unto him, "You must recant to-day, whether you will or will not ; otherwise I will condemn all your theses for the reason assigned above." But Luther did not recant. He concluded the interview with the request to grant him a few days more for further consideration.

On the same day Staupitz also arrived in Augsburg. All action now taken was first deliberated over in common. Luther submitted a written declaration, offering publicly to defend his theses, and prepared to receive the judgment of the faculties at Basel, Freiburg, Louvain, and Paris upon them. Cajetan smiled at this proposal, and admonished him to give up such idle thoughts, but rather to reflect upon his course and to retreat, for he would find it "hard to kick against the pricks !" In no case would he admit of a disputation ; but he permitted Luther to submit another and a longer explanation of the principal points at issue.

This document was sent to Cajetan on the following day. In it Luther emphatically declares : that the papal

decretals may err and conflict with Holy Writ ; that
every individual Christian can exercise the right to
prove the papal decisions in the light of God's Word ;
and in conclusion, Luther entreats the legate to show
him a better way, and not to force him to act contrary to
his conscience, for we must obey God rather than man.
The cardinal legate rejected Luther's written declarations without examination, and again urged him to recant, whereupon a violent war of words ensued.   The
cardinal threatened with ban and interdict, and dismissed
Luther, saying, "Go, and do not show your face again
to me, unless it be to recant."

Thus was Luther sent away by the cardinal, who is
said to have added this remark : "I will not confer with
this beast again, for it has deep eyes and wonderful
speculations in its head."   Staupitz and Link now departed from the city of Augsburg, not believing it to be
safe to trust the Italians.   But Luther tarried and
awaited the pleasure of the legate.   The latter, however, remained silent, even after Luther had written
again in a humble spirit asking forgiveness for his exhib-
ited violence, promising to remain silent if his opponents
would do the same, and professing himself as willing to
recant, provided he were better instructed.   But although he made all these concessions, he received no answer.   And after he had drawn up another declaration,
appealing from "the badly informed Pope to the better-
to-be-instructed Pope," he sent it to Cajetan, and nailed
a copy of it to the door of the cathedral.   He then left
the city on the 20th of October.

Luther's friends, fearing that he would not be permitted to depart from the city, provided for him a
horse and an old companion at arms, and dismissed him
at night through a secret gate in the city walls.   Thus he

escaped upon a hard-riding trotter, in his monk's coat, without boots or pants, spurs or sword, travelling about forty miles before he sought rest. When he dismounted at the inn at Monheim* he could hardly stand, and for weariness fell down upon the straw. In Gräfenthal † he met the friendly Count Albert of Mansfeld, who laughed at Luther's feats of riding, and invited him to join his company.

On the anniversary day of the nailing of the theses to the church door, Luther returned to Wittenberg amid the rejoicings of students and citizens. In the evening he sent a message to his friend Spalatin, saying, " By God's grace I have arrived safe and sound, but uncertain how long I shall remain. For my cause is so situated that I both hope and fear. I am filled with joy and peace, so that I am surprised that the trials which have befallen me should appear to many to be something great."

In possession of inward joy and peace, and surrounded by the circle of his friends at Wittenberg, Luther could now continue the conflict against the papacy. Soon there arrived a letter from the cardinal, Cajetan, preferring charges against Luther, and demanding his surrender or expulsion from Wittenberg. But the Elector Frederick did not accede to this demand. He carefully protected Luther, and insisted upon it that the controversy should be settled in Germany. Privately he felt a warm interest in Luther's cause, but desired that he should desist from further provocation.

Yet Luther did not refrain from new measures and continued declarations. He published a report of his

* Augsburg and Monheim are in Bavaria.
† Gräfenthal is in the Thuringian Forest.

interviews with Cajetan, and added a farther justification
of his procedure, in which he more positively than
ever before attacked the papacy. The doctrine of the
divine right of the papacy and of its necessary existence
as an essential part of the Church of Christ, he declared to be "the foolishness of silly people, who in opposition to Christ's own words, that 'the kingdom of God
cometh not with observation,' would bind the church of
Christ to time and place ; and who would dare question
the Christian standing of any one not disposed to submit
to the Pope's domination."

Shortly thereafter Luther appealed, in a formal and
solemn proclamation, to a universal council of the Christian Church. By this act he forever severed his relations
to the papacy. Daily he expected to receive the ban of excommunication from Rome. He made all necessary preparations, in order, as he wrote to Spalatin, that he might
be ready, on the arrival of the ban, to go out like Abraham,
not knowing whither, but certain that God is everywhere.
In one of his sermons he said to the congregation : " I
am now a very uncertain preacher, as you have already
experienced, and have often gone off without bidding
you farewell. If that should happen again, you may
take my present words as a farewell greeting, in case I
should not return." He was prepared each moment for
flight and exile. He felt also that he must withdraw for
the Elector's sake, in order that no suspicion should at-
tach itself to the latter because of any supposed adherence
to Luther's teachings upon indulgences and the papal
authority. He also thought if he remained at Wittenberg, that he could not speak and write as freely as he
would desire, whereas if he departed he could freely deliver himself and offer his life unto Christ. He was filled
with courage for the conflict and with the spirit of action.

'Far more extensive issues are being born of my pen,"
writes Luther; "I do not know whence these thoughts
come; in my opinion this movement has not yet fairly
begun, instead of soon ending, as the noble lords at Rome
vainly imagine." "The more they rage and meditate
upon the use of force, the less do I fear, and the more
freely will I attack the Roman serpents. I am prepared
for the worst that may happen and await the counsel of
God." "This I know, indeed; that I would be treated
as the dearest and most agreeable person, did I but speak
one word : *revoco;* that is, I recall. But I will not make
myself a heretic by the recall of that opinion by which
I became a Christian. I would rather die, be burnt,
exiled, and accursed."

But the danger from Rome did not threaten as speedily
as was anticipated or feared. The project there entertained, of bringing the rebellious monk back to a state
of obedience, had not been given up; but the time had
not yet come for extreme measures.

Karl von Miltitz, a Saxon nobleman and chamberlain of
the Pope, was now sent as an ambassador to Germany,
with special instructions to the Elector of Saxony. In
the person of the latter the papal chair recognized the
secret protector of the dangerous monk. The mission
of Miltitz was to deprive Luther of his patron's support,
and then to lead him away to Rome.

To this end the papal ambassador appeared before the
Elector, presenting him with a distinguished emblem of
gracious favor, the golden rose. This was "a very
precious and mysterious present," which the Pope was
accustomed annually to bestow upon that eminent Christian prince who had rendered good service to the apostolic authority, the Pope at Rome. Miltitz was commis-
sioned to present this golden rose to the Elector of

Saxony, to the intent that the divine fragrance of this flower should penetrate the heart of Frederick, so that he might receive the requests of the ambassador with a pious regard, and be disposed with glowing ardor to carry out the sacred wishes of the Pope. At least this much was expected in Rome from the fragrance of the golden rose. Irreverent wits remarked, that if the rose had arrived sooner in Wittenberg its perfume would have been more agreeable ; for it had lost its fragrance on the long and wearisome journey !

Miltitz was empowered to demand the following, as expressed in a special communication : the Elector should support Miltitz in the measures to be taken against Luther, the child of Satan and the son of perdition, because of his heretical preaching in the lands of Frederick. Messages of similar import were addressed to Spalatin, the magistrate of Wittenberg, and to many others. It is said that Miltitz was armed with more than seventy such papal communications.

At the close of December Miltitz* arrived in Altenburg. Well acquainted as he was with the condition of affairs in Germany, he had informed himself on the way, among the cultured as well as among the common people, in regard to the popular opinion of the man against whom he had been sent. He soon found that out of every five

---

* Miltitz had made an appointment to meet Tetzel at Altenburg, in Saxony, to reprimand him for his excesses. But the latter, fearing the popular wrath, did not dare to undertake the journey. After Miltitz had concluded his conference with Luther, he went to Leipsic, and meeting Tetzel he administered so severe a reproof that he sickened and died of chagrin in a Dominican cloister, July 4th, 1519. Luther wrote Tetzel a comforting letter during his sickness—an evidence of the nobility of soul and large-heartedness of the great Reformer.

persons, scarce two or three had remained loyal to Rome.
It is possible that because of this discovery he changed
his method of procedure, for he confessed that he
would not have dared to take Luther away with him to
Rome, not even if he had had an army of 25,000 men.

In Altenburg Miltitz met Luther in the first week of
the new year, 1519. He addressed Luther amid tears
and with many words, exhorting him to recant, and
showing all possible friendship and affection. He hoped
in this way to persuade Luther. But Luther did not trust
him. This apparent good-will seemed to him hypocritical; the greeting, a Judas's kiss; the lamentations, croc-
odile's tears ! Yet he promised to make concessions so
far as his conscience would permit him to do, but certainly nothing more. They mutually agreed, furthermore,
"that both parties should be forbidden to write and to
teach upon the questions at issue." Besides this, Miltitz
proposed to write to the Pope, requesting him to appoint
a learned bishop to act as arbitrator, having in mind the
Archbishop of Treves (Trier). The joint meeting was to
be held hereafter in the city of Coblentz.

Thus far the negotiations seem to have taken a favorable turn. Luther, likewise, addressed a meek epistle to
the Pope. He also published an address to the German
people, in which he seeks to refute the slanders of those
who had endeavored to prejudice him and his cause by
misrepresenting his teachings about intercession, purgatory, indulgences, the commands of the Holy Church,
good works, and the Roman Church ; he aims to show,
that in no wise does he depart from the faith of all
Christendom ; that in order to maintain peace he is
willing to make sacrifices ; and he also professes his belief in certain Roman Catholic teachings which he afterward publicly rejected.

Miltitz seems to have been satisfied with these declarations of Luther, though it could not yet be known how they would be regarded by the Papal authorities. Further negotiations to induce Luther to go to Coblentz were unsuccessful, for he would not venture to undergo the risk upon an uncertainty, and hence declined. He pleasantly remarked that he had not so much time to spare to take so long a promenade ! Besides, the Archbishop of Treves had received no mandate from Rome to hold the proposed conference meeting.

In the meanwhile the Emperor Maximilian * had died, and the Elector of Saxony had become Imperial Vicar, an event which exercised a favorable influence upon Luther's cause. The papal authorities were obliged, now more than ever, to take the Elector into account in all their plans, for his position in Germany exercised a determining influence. The successor of Maximilian was his nineteen-year-old nephew, King Charles † of Spain. He was no friend to German life and institutions. Luther and his cause experienced this on more than one occasion.

* Maximilian I. was of the House of Hapsburg, born in 1459, and died in 1519. He became Emperor of Germany in 1493.

† Charles I. of Spain, better known as Charles V., Emperor of Germany, was born in 1500, and died in 1558. He was chosen Emperor in 1519, and retired into a convent in 1556, his brother Ferdinand succeeding him as Emperor of Germany.

CHAPTER VI.

WHILST Miltitz continued his attempts at reconciliation and prepared the way for a meeting between Luther and the Archbishop of Treves, Luther felt himself obliged to get ready for a public debate with Dr. Eck.* The latter had been carrying on an epistolary war with one of Luther's colleagues, Dr. Karlstadt. This was now to be ended by a public disputation at Leipsic. To this end Dr. Eck published a number of theses which he proposed to defend against Karlstadt. But in these theses Luther was attacked, rather than his colleague, especially in regard to the supremacy of the Pope in the early centuries of the Christian Church. On this point Karlstadt had neither written nor spoken. Hence it was evident that Eck's theses were directed against Luther, who felt himself obliged once more to enter the arena of conflict. Since he had been attacked by Eck he demanded the right to take part in the debate. His friends endeavored to dissuade him from this step, but he soon convinced them that he must go himself and defend his cause, saying: "Even should I perish, the world will not go to destruction on that account. By the grace of God the Wittenbergers [meaning his adherents] have so far progressed that they do not need me."

* John Mayr von Eck was born in Eck, Swabia, in 1486, and died in Ingolstadt, in Bavaria, in 1543. The latter part of his life was devoted to effect a reunion of the conflicting parties.

The disputation was appointed for the 27th of June, 1519. Duke George of Saxony came from Dresden to Leipsic and ordered the largest hall in his palace, the Pleissenburg, to be used for that purpose, and handsomely decorated. Dr. Eck arrived in time ; the Wittenbergers, on Friday, June 24th. " The latter entered by the Grimma gate," thus writes an eye-witness, " escorted by 200 of their students, armed with spears and halberds. Dr. Karlstadt rode first, followed by Luther and Melanchthon in an open wagon. After they had entered the Grimma gate and had reached the doors of St. Paul's church cemetery, Dr. Karlstadt's wagon broke down, and the doctor was thrown into the mud. Dr. Martinus and his companion, Philippus, rode by and continued their course. The people that saw it remarked : " Luther will triumph, but Karlstadt will be defeated."

The day before the appointed time, it was agreed upon that Karlstadt and Eck should open the debate. On the 27th of June the disputation was inaugurated with great secular and religious festivities, beginning with an address of welcome in Latin, continuing with a mass in St. Thomas's church, and concluding with a musical concert. A large number of theologians, as well as educated and uneducated laymen, had assembled to attend the proceedings. During four days Eck and Karlstadt contended about theological questions of the free-will of man and his relation to the operations of divine grace. Eck had the advantage over Karlstadt, both in dialectic ability and in power of memory. The members of the University of Leipsic supported Eck and exalted him in every possible way. But Luther and his Wittenberg associates they regarded at a distance. Between the students of the two universities violent contentions arose upon the questions at issue.

On the 4th of July the debate began between Luther
and Eck. A contemporary and eye-witness has preserved
the following sketch of the contending parties : " Martin
Luther is of medium stature, meagre in body, and so exhausted by his cares and studies that one can almost count
every bone in his frame.   He is as yet in the strength of
manhood.   His voice is clear and distinct ; his learning
and knowledge of the Scriptures are wonderful, so that
he has full command.

" He understands Greek and Hebrew well enough to
judge of different interpretations of the Scriptures.   Nor
is he lacking in material for his discourses, for he has possession of an extraordinary amount of facts and words.
In social life and intercourse he is polite and friendly ;
there is nothing gloomy or proud about him ; and he has
the disposition to accommodate himself to different persons and varying circumstances.   In society he is cheerful and witty.   He is always lively, joyful, and positive,
and has a pleasing countenance, no matter how hard his
opponents threaten him ; so much so that one is obliged
to believe that the man cannot bear so heavy a burden
without the help of the gods.   By many he is reproached
with being intemperate in his attacks and biting in his
criticisms, more so indeed than is becoming to a theologian,
and to one who is presenting something new in divine
things.   In the case of Karlstadt all these characteristics
are very much reduced in degree ; he is smaller in stature, his face is dark and sunburnt, his voice hollow and
disagreeable.   Eck, on the contrary, is tall, well-built, and
robust, has a full round voice proceeding from a large
chest, well-endowed either for an actor or a town-crier.
His features are such that he would sooner be taken for
a butcher or a soldier than for a theologian.   His memory is excellent, and if his understanding were likewise,

he would be regarded as a perfect work of nature. But he is lacking in quick perceptive faculties and in acuteness of judgment. His aim is to adduce a large amount of stuff, to mystify his hearers, and to produce the impression of great superiority. To this must be added his incredible audacity, for as soon as he observes that he has been caught in the net of his opponent, he seeks to turn the discussion into another channel. And then he possesses great vivacity in speaking and shouting, and freedom in gesticulating with the arms and the whole body.''

The debate had reached its climax when Luther referred to the theses of Huss, condemned by the Council of Constance, in 1415, and in bad repute all over Germany. Eck endeavored to throw the suspicion of sympathy with the Bohemian heresy upon Luther, in discussing the question, whether the supremacy of the Pope was based upon divine or human right. But Luther guarded himself well, and yet maintained that among the articles of Huss there were many that were Christian and evangelical, such as these : that there is but one universal Christian Church ; and that the belief in the supremacy of the Roman Catholic Church is not necessary to salvation. Whilst Luther was thus quoting the theses of Huss,* Duke George cried out with a loud voice, audible to all, '' May the deuce take that !'' shaking his head and planting his arms at his sides. At another time, when Luther declared that the Pope derives his authority not by divine but by human right, Duke George again exclaimed, '' The Pope *is* Pope, whether

---

* Duke George of Saxony remained all his life-time one of the bitterest opponents of Luther and the Reformation. He persecuted and punished his own subjects for espousing the new doctrines. At his death, in 1539, his brother Henry succeeded him and formally introduced Protestantism.

by human or by divine right." The debate upon the chief question, the supremacy of the Pope, was continued for five days, but without any result. Further disputations concerning purgatory, indulgence, and repentance were of minor importance ; likewise the closing debate between Eck and Karlstadt. On the 15th of July the disputation was closed. Eck claimed the victory. He departed with a display of triumph, extolled by his friends, and rewarded with favor and honors by Duke George of Saxony. Luther left for home in ill-humor. He thus expresses himself about the Leipsic disputation : "Eck and his friends did not seek truth, but fame. No wonder, then, that the debate had a bad beginning and worse ending."

But in truth this disputation was very helpful to the dissemination of Reformation thoughts. Everywhere the questions at issue were discussed. "Luther's teachings," writes a contemporary, "have aroused so much strife, dissension, and disturbance among the people, that there is scarce a country or a city, a village or a family, that has not been divided and agitated even unto blows."

CHAPTER VII.

ANOTHER interval of time had elapsed. Luther had once more returned to Wittenberg and zealously devoted himself to his work in the professor's chair as well as in the pulpit, where he clearly and impressively proclaimed the new truths. In his writings, too, he was not idle. And herein a new controversy developed itself.

As yet the Pope had passed no public sentence of condemnation upon Luther, although he had often called him a heretic deserving his anathema. The universities of Cologne and Louvain, as well as the Bishop of Meissen, now brought their complaints against Luther before the Pope. The former maintained that Luther's writings should be destroyed by fire, and he himself forced to recant. The latter called attention to a passage in one of Luther's pamphlets, in which he contended that the Church should again grant the cup (the wine) to the laity in the Lord's Supper. For, why should the priest be entitled to more than the layman? Christ knows of no such difference. In his profound study of the Scriptures this conviction had grown upon him, and in this point of doctrine he found himself in accord with Huss and his followers. He was now stigmatized as a fellow-heretic with Huss; but he was not much troubled about it. He replied to these accusations as follows: "All that I have thus far taught, I have learned from

John Huss *—but without knowing it. John Staupitz
has done the same. In short, we are all Hussites, without being aware of it. The Apostle Paul and Augustine
were also Hussites ! For fear and trembling, I do not
know what to think of the impending judgments of God
upon men, who, for more than one hundred years, have
condemned the clearest evangelical truth, and have
suffered no one to declare it.'' And at another time he
wrote to Spalatin : '' Do not imagine that Christ's cause
upon earth can be furthered in sweet peace. The word
of holiness can never be proclaimed without unrest and
danger ; it is a word of eternal majesty, and accom-
plishes great things and wonderful, among the high and
the great. It kills, as says the prophet, the fat and the
strong in Israel (Ezekiel xxxiv. 16). In this matter peace
must be given up or else the word of God denied. The
war is the Lord's, who came not to bring peace into the
world. If thou dost rightly estimate the Gospel, then
do not believe that its cause can be conducted without
tumult, offence, and disturbance. The word of God is
a sword ; it is war, overthrow, vexation, poison. It will
meet the children of Ephraim, as Amos (v. 19) says, like
a bear in the way and a lion in the woods.'' And concerning himself Luther says : '' I cannot deny that I
am more violent than I ought to be ; they know that,
and for that very reason ought not to have excited the
dog ! How hard it is to temper the heat and restrain

* John Huss, the Bohemian Reformer, was born in 1373, and
burned at the stake July 6th, 1415. On his way to the place of
execution he uttered this memorable prophecy : '' You are to-day
roasting a lean goose (the meaning of his name) ; but after a hundred years you will hear the song of a swan, arising from my
ashes, whom you will not be able to roast.'' Hence the swan is
often found in pictures of Luther.

the pen, thou knowest from personal experience. This is the reason why I have always been unwilling publicly to proclaim my cause. And the more I am disposed not to do so, the more I am compelled against my will ; and this happens because of the severest accusations which are heaped upon God's word and myself. And so shameful has this been, that even if my pen and my impetuosity had not carried me away, a heart of stone would have been moved to take up arms ; how much the more I that am impetuous by nature, and possess not a very dull pen !''

Luther soon had ample opportunity to set his pen in motion. The entire Dominican order exerted its influence against Luther. Eck hastened to Rome to work against him. The Bishop of Brandenberg in a moment of excitement is said to have remarked that he would not place his head to rest until he had thrown Martin Luther into the fire ! Duke George of Saxony, shocked at Luther's agreement with the Hussites, preferred charges against him before his own ruler, the Elector of Saxony. In short, mighty enemies appeared from all quarters, bent upon his destruction.

As yet the Elector protected him. And from many other parties did Luther receive active support. His writings were scattered broadcast, in hundreds of copies, all over the land, gaining for him many friends and adherents. Many who had formerly been at enmity with Rome now united their cause and fortunes with his own. But the most renowned among the learned of his times, Erasmus and Reuchlin, prudently kept in the background. On the other hand, Ulrich von Hutten, a German knight, espoused Luther's cause with bolder courage and a powerful activity. Daring and spirited, he wielded a vigorous pen, and was prepared to serve the Gospel with his sword. He glowed with ardor for the honor and greatness of Germany, and hated the Italian spirit. From early youth he was an enemy to monkery, and by his boldness he inflicted many a blow upon the papacy. Among the circle of his friends and equals he secured numerous supporters for Luther's cause. At first he regarded the advent of the Augustinian as a pitiable, monkish quarrel ; but soon he was better informed. After many wanderings and manifold experiences he found at last an energetic and powerful friend in the person of Franz von Sickingen, experienced in war and informed as to political questions. Ulrich von Hutten now united his fortunes with the latter in order to make common cause against the obscurantists and the Roman hierarchy. Landstuhl and Ebernburg were the names of the strong castles of Franz von Sickingen, which could afford a safe protection to the oppressed. As such they were now offered to the bold monk who had attacked the papacy with so keen weapons. Should the ban of excommunication arrive, and should Luther no longer be safe in Wittenberg, then Sickingen's burg would afford an excellent place of refuge. And another knight, Sylvester von Schauenburg, wrote to him : " Should the Elector and others in authority demand of you to recede, do not let that trouble you ; nor do you take refuge among the Bohemians ; for I and hundreds of the nobility will protect you from danger."

Such messages must have been highly welcome to Luther. " Schauenburg and Sickingen," * said he, " have

* Schauenburg was a native and inhabitant of Holstein. Sickingen was one of the last of the German knights who maintained the right of private warfare. He was noted for his valor and generosity. He died in 1523, of a wound received in defending

delivered me from the fear of men. I shall now have to encounter the wrath of demons." He wished that the Pope be informed that he, Luther, would now find protection from the shafts of his lightnings in the heart of Germany ; and that, thus protected, he would attack the Romanists in a manner far different from that in which he had been able to attack them in his official position. " My opponents shall know," wrote Luther, "that what I have not yet said against them has been owing, not to my leniency, nor to their merit or tyranny, but to the name and fame of the Elector and the common interests of the University of Wittenberg. As far as I am concerned, the die is cast ! Rome's favor and wrath are contemned ! I will never become reconciled to them, nor hold fellowship with them. Let them condemn and burn my books !"

But Luther's adherents, and especially Ulrich von Hutten,* said, " What have we to do with the Romans and with their bishop ? Have we not archbishops and bishops in Germany ? As if we were obliged to kiss the feet of the Pope ! Let Germany return, and it will return, to its own bishops and shepherds !"

" The time for silence is passed, and the time for speaking is come." Thus Luther begins his pamphlet, " To the Christian Nobles of the German Nation : About

his castle Landstuhl, near Kaiserslautern, in the Palatinate. His other stronghold, Ebernburg, is now a picturesque ruin on the Rhine.

* Hutten was born near Fulda in 1488, and died in Switzerland in 1523. He was placed in a cloister to become a monk, but ran away and led a short, wandering, and tempestuous career. His intense national spirit, his bitter enmity against Rome, and his caustic satires upon the immoral and superstitious clergy, aided the cause of the Reformation.

the Reformation of Christendom." He now appeals to
the laity, in the hope that God will use them to deliver His
Church, since the clergy have become altogether indif-
ferent. Not through wantonness or temerity does he
presume to address the Emperor and Christian nobles of
the German nation ; but the need and the grievances
which afflict all classes in Christendom, and especially in
Germany, compel him to cry out and to ask whether God
would grant the Spirit to some one to extend the help-
ing hand to miserable humanity.

" The Romanists," says Luther, " have with great
adroitness built a triple wall about themselves, so that no
one has been able to reform them, and because of which
all Christendom has fearfully'degenerated. In the first
place, whenever they have been threatened by the secular power, they have resisted and said, The secular power
has no right over the spiritual power ; but, on the contrary, the latter has control over the former. And when
the Holy Scripture was brought to bear upon them, they
contended that the Pope alone should interpret it. And,
in the third place, when they are threatened with a
council, they pretend that no one but the Pope can call
a council. Thus have they secretly stolen three of our
rods, that they may go unpunished ; and having fortified
themselves with this triple wall, they have carried on
their knavery and wickedness in security."

These three walls Luther now proposes to overturn and
demolish. He declares the difference between the spiritual and secular orders to be fictitious and hypocritical ; he
maintains that all Christians belong to the spiritual order,
and that there is no difference between them other than
that of the respective offices which different members have
wherewith to serve one another, according to 1 Peter ii. 9
and Rev. iii. 10. The secular power is not superior to

the spiritual power.   The former is entitled to rule free
and unhindered upon its own territory.   No Pope or
bishop herein can interfere ; no priest is exempt from its
control.   The second wall is even weaker and more un-
safe, for they pretend to be masters of Scripture, when
during their whole lives they have learned nothing from
it.   Christ has said of all Christians that they should be
taught of God.   So that even an obscure man, if he be a
true Christian, may have the right understanding of the
Bible.   And, on the other hand, the Pope, if he be not
a true Christian, will not be taught of God.   If the
Pope were always and alone right, then we ought to
pray, "I believe in the Pope of Rome."   The Christian Church would thus, as it were, be concentrated into
one person, which would be nothing else than satanic
and infernal error.   The third wall, however, falls with
the first two ; for where the Pope acts contrary to the
Scriptures, we are in duty bound to stand by the word of
God and to admonish Him according to Christ's command :
" If thy brother shall trespass against thee, go and tell him
his fault, between thee and him alone" (Matt. xviii. 15).
But if he is to be accused before the church, then the
church must be convened in a council, which should be
a free Christian council, bound by no vow to the Pope,
nor by any so-called canonical law, but subject only to
God's word in the Holy Scriptures.

Luther then considers in detail the several points upon
which the council is to act, and concerning which a
reformation must be insisted upon.   He calls the Pope
the antichrist.   He contrasts his self-exaltation, his
worldly pride, the idolatry practised with him, with the
life and person of Christ, who went about in poverty, and
offered himself a sacrifice on the cross.   He considers at
length the tyranny exercised by the Roman court over

the local state churches, and especially over those of
Germany, in frequent extortions.   The churches of each
country should be permitted to regulate their own affairs
at home.   Then he protests against the haughty and
insolent behavior of the Pope towards the German
Emperor, in presuming to control the latter, obliging
him to hold his stirrup and kiss his foot ! In his spiritual
office, in preaching, in dispensing the word of divine
grace, the Pope is indeed superior to the Emperor ; but
in all other things the Emperor is superior.   Luther
demands, furthermore, the abolition of the state of celi-
bacy for the clergy ; restriction of the system of monasticism, of festivals and holidays, as well as of pil-
grimages ; organization of charitable work, and the
erection of schools for boys and girls.   He is deeply dis-
tressed when he regards the condition of the youth, who,
in the very centre of Christendom, are languishing in
ignorance and going to destruction in sin.   And after
touching upon many other questions, such as the extor-
tionate charges and usurious interest in the loaning of
money, he concludes : "I am well aware that I have
sung in too lofty a strain, and have said many things in
vain, attacking other things also too sharply.   But what
shall I do ? I am at least obliged to express my opinion.
If I were able I would also do that which I claim should be
done.   I would rather have the world angry at me than
have God angry.   They can deprive me of nothing more
than my life.   I have often offered peace to my opponents, but God has obliged me to open my mouth
wider and give them enough to do to speak and to
write, to bark and to cry.   There is one more song that
I can sing ; if they are itching for it they shall hear it,
and in the loudest strains."   And his closing words
are : "God give us all a Christian understanding, and

especially to the Christian nobles of the German nation a right spiritual courage, to do the very best for our poor Church.   Amen.''

In the course of a few weeks, in the month of August, 1520, four thousand copies of this "war-trumpet" were circulated, and Luther was obliged to publish a new edition. Besides this, he also wrote a series of pamphlets for instruction and consolation.   He wielded a ready pen. "I have surely a rapid hand and a quick memory," says Luther, "so that what I write flows freely of its own account, and not as if I had to produce it ; and yet I am not able to get over the ground."

As to the new song he wished to sing of Rome, he no doubt referred to his treatise about "The Babylonian Captivity of the Church."   In this he speaks, with clearness and deep religious fervor, of the meaning of the Sacraments. But he opposes the so-called sacraments of confirmation, marriage, ordination, and supreme unction.   At the close he says : "I hear that the papal anathemas are ready to be hurled against me to compel me to recant. If this be so, then I wish that this little book be considered a part of my future recantation, in order that they may not vainly complain about their inflated tyranny. And in a little while I will issue a recantation, by the help of Christ, the like of which the Roman court has hitherto neither seen nor heard, and therewith I shall prove my obedience, in the name of my Lord Jesus Christ.   Amen !"

CHAPTER VIII.

WHAT had long been anticipated now came to pass. Eck arrived in Germany with the papal bull of excommunication. On the 21st of September, 1520, he published it in Meissen. It was also proclaimed elsewhere. In the beginning of October it was published in Wittenberg.

The papal bull begins as follows : "Arise, O Lord, and judge thy cause ! Remember the reproach which the foolish cast against Thee all day long ! St. Peter, St. Paul, the congregation of saints, and the whole church are called upon to arise. The foxes would lay waste the vineyard of the Lord ; a wild boar has entered therein ; a savage beast would pasture there." Then forty-one of Luther's theses are considered and condemned as heretical. He himself is called upon to recant within sixty days. If he and his followers refuse, they will be treated as stiff-necked heretics. His writings are to be burned, so that his remembrance shall be totally blotted out of the congregation of Christian believers. All intercourse with him and his adherents is forbidden. Every one is commanded to seize Martin Luther and to deliver him to the Pope in Rome. There he shall be dealt with according to law. Without doubt the punishment intimated refers to death at the stake, for the papal bull expressly condemns the declaration of Luther : to burn heretics is against the will of the Holy Spirit.

Luther himself received the papal interdict with great calmness of soul. What next would happen he did not know; he intrusted it to Him whose throne is in the heavens, and who had foreseen this event, its beginning and ending, from all eternity. He had but little hope in the good-will of the Emperor. "Would that Charles were a man," he cried out, "and that he would contend for Christ and against Satan." He called to mind the Biblical saying, "Put not your trust in princes" (Ps. cxlvi. 3). "They are but men, and cannot help you. If the Gospel were of such a nature that it could be diffused and supported by the great men of this world, then God would not have intrusted it to fishermen."

Eck, however, was badly received, with his bull, in Germany. In Leipsic the citizens posted warnings against him on every street-corner. To save himself from personal violence he was obliged to take refuge in the monastery of St. Paul's church. The students sang satirical songs for his benefit. He did not meet with better treatment in Erfurt, where the students, arms in hand, made an attack upon him, seized the printed copies of the bull, and threw them into the river Gera. Miltitz was nevertheless encouraged to resume his attempts at reconciliation between the Pope and Luther. And notwithstanding the bull of excommunication, he did not doubt that the conflict could be allayed. By the advice of the Elector, Luther agreed to make another effort, and directed a letter to Pope Leo, inclosing a new treatise, upon the Liberty of the Christian, comprehending the substance of Christian life. And thus does Luther declare himself : " A Christian is a free man over all things, and subject to no man. No external things can make him pious and free, but the holy Gospel only, and a strong, pure faith in God and Jesus Christ.

Through this a Christian is exalted above all things, and
made his own master. Nothing can injure his salvation ;
everything must be subject to him and to his salvation.
Who can perfectly conceive the honor and the supreme
elevation of a Christian ? Through his kingdom he con-
trols all earthly things ; through his priesthood he con-
trols God, for God does what he asks and wills.''

But, on the other hand, a Christian is also a ministering
servant in all things and subject to every one. For he
has still another will in his flesh that would lead him
captive in sin. Hence he dare not be idle. He must
labor with himself to expel his evil desires and to subdue his own body. Nor dare we despise the weakness
or the weak faith of our neighbor, but must serve him
in all things to his improvement. Thus the Christian,
who is a free man, becomes a ministering servant in all
things and subject to every one. And at the close he says :
'' A Christian does not live unto himself, but in Christ
and in his neighbor : in Christ through faith, in his
neighbor through love. Through faith he rises above
himself into God ; from God he returns again among his
own through love, and yet always remains in God and in
divine love.''

This treatise is one of the finest that came from Luther's
pen. It stands on a level with and is equal to the other
two famous Reformation treatises, '' To the Christian
Nobles of the German Nation'' and '' The Babylonian
Captivity of the Church.'' It is a glorious testimony
showing that, in spite of the Pope's anathema, his soul
was resting confidently in God. And hence he could
write to the Pope : '' From this treatise his Holiness
might perceive how he (Luther) would rather be engaged,
and much more profitably indeed, were he not hindered
by impious papal flatterers.''

In the papal bull he found his teachings misrepresent-
ed. Hence he wrote another treatise entitled, "Against
the Bulls of the Antichrist." Again he appealed to a
council of the Church, as he had done two years before
this, but from a different standpoint, and with a conscious
certainty of the justice of his cause.

In the meanwhile the judgment of the papal bull was
executed upon Luther's writings, in the city of Cologne
and in the presence of the Emperor. In Louvain and
Mayence they were also publicly burned.

Luther hesitated no longer. On the 10th of November,
1520, he publicly announced that the bull of excommunication and the papal books of canonical law would be
burned on the following morning at nine o'clock. At the
appointed time, students, masters, and doctors were
assembled at the designated place, at the Elster Gate,
near the Augustinian monastery. A Master, i.e. an advanced student, prepared the place, piled on the fagots,
and applied the fire. Then Luther cast the Roman
decretals, together with the papal bull, into the flames,
exclaiming, "Because thou hast offended the Holy One
of the Lord, be thou consumed with everlasting fire."

This being accomplished, Luther returned with his
friends to the city. Several hundred students remained
at the fire feeding the flames with papal writings. Others
paraded the streets, deriding Eck and the papal bull.

On the following day, after the opening lecture at the
university, Luther earnestly addressed his hearers, warning them to beware of papal laws and statutes. To
burn the Pope's decretals was mere child's play. Far
more important and necessary would it be to burn the
Pope, i.e. the Roman authority, with all its teachings
and abominations. "If ye do not," said he, "with all
your heart, resist the blasphemous government of the

Pope, ye cannot be saved. For the Pope's dominion is so contrary to Christ's kingdom and to the Christian life, that it would be safer and better to live in an uninhabited desert than to dwell in an anti-Christian empire. To Staupitz, who had retired to Salzburg, he wrote that in burning the Pope's bull he at first feared and trembled. But now he rejoiced as at no other act of his life. Luther, by these proceedings, had formally severed his ecclesiastical relations with the Church of Rome. To complete this act also externally, he now released himself from the obligations of monastic laws.

But by his bold actions he had let loose a storm which raged over all Germany—a storm which could not be quieted until the Judgment Day. Thus were the ruling spirits excited on both sides of the question. Germany was divided into two hostile camps, that fought each other most violently, with pictures and in writings, with biting satire and in sober earnestness. In the German nation, complains a contemporary, there prevailed such controversy, disturbance, and disorder that no kingdom, no city, no village, and no house was free from this quarrel, but all were divided, the one against the other. Everywhere excitement and bitter feeling! Here and there wonderful, horrible stories were reported about wars and insurrections! Ulrich von Hutten had really purposed to resort to arms to assist the Gospel with the sword, and to drive the Romanists from the land. But Luther restrained him, saying, "We must not contend for the Gospel with brute force and murder. Through the Word the world has been overcome ; through the Word the Church has been preserved ; through the Word the Church will be purified and restored."

The time allotted for recantation had expired. On the

3d of January, 1521, Pope Leo issued another bull against Luther and his adherents. But the papal authority had been so completely weakened that the anathema and interdict were received in Germany with shouts of laughter.

CHAPTER IX.

IT was on the 16th of April, 1521, at 10 o'clock in the morning, that the watchman upon the tower of the cathedral at Worms on the Rhine signalled the approach of a strange cavalcade. At the head rode the herald, with the insignia of the imperial eagle upon his breast. In an open wagon followed Dr. Martin Luther, in his monk's attire, with three companions, surrounded by a great array of stately riders, who had joined him on the way or had gone out from the city to meet him. Thousands had hurriedly gathered from all sides to view the procession as it entered the city, to behold the daring Augustinian monk who would appear before the Emperor and the Imperial Diet. Young and old, high and low, crowded to see him. Mothers lifted their infants high into the air. A great multitude of people surged about the wagon and the accompanying horsemen. And thus they proceeded together to the mansion of the Knights of St. John, where Luther secured lodgment. As he descended from the wagon he remarked, "God will be with me."

Not for a moment had Luther ever been in doubt what he would do if summoned to appear before the Emperor. "When I am called," said he, "I will ride there sick if I cannot go well; for I dare not doubt that the Lord calls if the Emperor desires me to do this.

And should they employ force, as seems likely—since they have not called me to afford better information—we must intrust ourselves to the hand of God. He that preserved His three servants in the fiery furnace of the King of Babylon still lives and reigns. If He will not preserve me, little does it matter, especially when we think of Christ, who, with so great ignominy, to the offence of all and the destruction of many, was put to death. But in this case, no reference is to be had to any one's danger, nor to any one's welfare, but solely to the cause of the Gospel, that it be not exposed to the scorn of the godless ; in order that our enemies be not given good cause to defame us, as if we dared not confess what we taught or were afraid to shed our blood on its behalf. May Christ, out of mercy, save us from such reproach, and save them from such glorying.''

Luther received the summons of the Emperor at the hands of the imperial herald, Caspar Sturm, of Oppenheim, on the 26th of March, 1521. He was to appear before the Emperor at Worms within twenty-one days, and a safe-conduct was assured him. The city council of Wittenberg provided wagon and horses for the journey. On the 2d of April, Tuesday after Easter, Luther departed for Worms, accompanied to the suburbs by his friends and colleagues and several hundred students. In bidding them farewell he admonished them, as his scholars, to hold fast to the pure doctrine of the Gospel. He took leave of his friend Melanchthon in the following words : ''Should I not return again, and should my enemies murder me, then I adjure thee, my dear brother, do not cease to teach, nor to adhere to, the truth of the Divine Word. Labor at the same time for me during my absence. Thou canst do it better than I. Hence there is not much lost if I am gone, so that

thou dost remain !   In thee our Lord God will yet have
a learned warrior.''

After he had taken a touching farewell of his friends,
who believed that they had seen him for the last time on
earth, he continued his journey by way of Leipsic,
Naumburg, Weimar, Erfurt, Gotha, and Eisenach.   In
the last named cities he preached.   The people of Erfurt
had prepared a festive and glorious reception ; they
went out of the city to meet him, and received him
with great enthusiasm.

At Eisenach, Luther's beloved city, he became very
sick.   Blood-letting was resorted to, and the burgomaster gave him some "noble water" (" edel Wäs-
serlein") to drink.   On the following day he continued
his journey, but all the way to Frankfort he felt very
much indisposed, more so than he had ever felt before.
Whenever he approached a city or town the people
flocked to see the wonderful man who had been so bold
as to oppose the Pope and all the world besides !   To
those, however, who warned him that he would speedily
be burned in Worms, as Huss had been in Constance, he
replied : "And even though they should kindle a fire
as high as heaven between Wittenberg and Worms, yet
would I go and appear in the name of the Lord ; yea, I
will confess Christ in the very mouth of Behemoth !''

As he was nearing the city of Worms, his friend
Spalatin, who was in the company of the Elector, sent
him a message warning him not to enter the city and to
incur so great danger.   Luther replied to him : " To
Worms was I called, and to Worms must I go.   And
were there as many devils there as tiles upon the roofs, yet
would I enter into that city.''   Sickingen invited him to
come to Castle Ebernburg, there to secure his life, and
to treat with the Emperor's confessor.   Luther declined

the invitation, saying: "Not to Ebernburg, but to
Worms have I been summoned. If the imperial confessor have aught to say to me, let him seek me there."
Moreover, he was obliged to hasten to reach Worms in
time before his safe-conduct had expired.

On the same day that he arrived in Worms he was
visited by a large number of the nobility, clergy, and
laity, until late at night. The Landgrave of Hesse also
called to see him, and in departing said, "If your
cause is a just one, Doctor, then may God assist you."

The Papists, on the other hand, sought to persuade his
Imperial Majesty to seize Luther and to put him to
death. They adduced the example of John Huss, and
said, "To a heretic one is under no obligation, either
to grant a safe-conduct or to keep it." But the Emperor
Charles replied, "Whatever promise has been made
must be fulfilled."

Early on the following morning the imperial marshal
notified Luther to appear at four o'clock in the afternoon,
in the presence of the Emperor, the Elector, and other
nobles of the empire, to hear why he had been ordered
to appear.

At the appointed time Luther was sent for. Before
going he sought comfort and strength in earnest prayer
to God. Then, with cheerful countenance, he followed the imperial marshal, by secret passage-ways, to
the assembly room of the episcopal palace, where the
Emperor lodged. The main street was impassable on
account of the great multitude of people that desired to
see him. Many had ascended to the roofs of the
houses, and vast throngs could with difficulty be kept
from the palace.

As Luther was passing to the assembly room of the diet,
a noted commander, George von Frundsberg, touched

him on the shoulder and said, "My dear monk, thou
art now about taking a step, the like of which neither
I nor many a commander on the hardest fought battle-field
has ever taken. If thou art right and sure of thy
cause, proceed in God's name, and be of good cheer;
God will not forsake thee."

After waiting for two hours, Luther was led into the
presence of the Imperial Diet. Here a glorious and
magnificent assemblage confronted him. In the centre
of the large hall the youthful Emperor, Charles V., was
enthroned under a purple canopy. Beside him was
seated his brother Ferdinand; behind him there stood a
glittering array of the nobles of the imperial court. To
the right and to the left of the throne, extending along
the walls, were seated two hundred princes and nobles of
the realm, ordered according to rank.

When Luther entered the hall a universal murmur of
excitement was heard. Order being restored, the imperial marshal, in the name of the Emperor, reminded
Luther that he must confine his answers to the pro-
pounded questions.

An official representative of the Archbishop of Treves
then addressed him as follows: "Martin Luther, his
sacred and invincible Majesty, with the advice and counsel of the nobility of the Roman Empire, has summoned
you to appear before his Majesty's throne, to demand an
answer to these two questions: First, do you acknowledge these books [heaped up on a bench at his side] to
be yours or not? And secondly, do you recant, or do you
adhere to and maintain, the contents of the same?"

Luther answered in a low voice, and as if he were
frightened, that the books were his, but whether he
should be prepared to defend or retract all alike would
be a question of faith, of his soul's salvation, and of God's

Word, which is the most precious treasure in heaven and on earth. In such a case he must not speak thoughtlessly. He therefore most humbly entreated his Imperial Majesty to grant him a respite for further consideration.

This was granted him until the next day, although with the rebuke that he had already had sufficient time for reflection.

On Thursday, the 18th of April, Luther was again · ordered to appear before the diet, but was obliged to wait amid a dense throng until six o'clock in the evening, before he was called into the presence of the Emperor. The same official that had addressed him on the previous day now demanded that he should give a final answer to the question whether he would defend all his books or withdraw some of them. Luther replied in a lengthy and well-considered address, modest in character and with great Christian joy and firmness. It could readily be seen that his books were not all alike. In some he had written about faith and good works, and in so simple and Christian a manner that even his opponents must confess that they were useful and innocent, and worthy to be read by Christian people. Such books he could not recall. The second kind were directed against the papacy and the papists, who were destroying all Christians, in body and soul, with their evil doctrine and example ; who had enslaved, burdened, and tortured the Christian conscience, and devoured the possessions of the German lands by incredible tyranny. If he were to retract these writings he would but strengthen this tyranny and make of himself a cloak of infamy to cover up all unchristian living and teaching. The third kind of books was of such as were written against individual persons who desired to defend Roman tyranny and destroy the gracious teachings of God. And these also he could not recall without

approving of the despotic papal rule. Citing the words
of Christ in his defence, " If I have spoken evil, bear
witness of the evil " (John 18 : 23), he asked for counter
testimony from the evangelical and prophetical writings.
If thus convinced, he would very readily and willingly recant all his alleged errors. He would then be the first
one to cast his writings into the flames.

Luther spoke in both German and Latin. After he
had finished, the princes held a short consultation.
Then the imperial representative reproached him for
having spoken disrespectfully, and for not having answered the proposed questions. He repelled Luther's
demand for counter-evidence, and maintained that his
heresies had been condemned by the Church and by its
general councils. What was now demanded of him was
a plain and straightforward answer, whether he would
or would not recant.

Thereupon Luther replied : " Since your Imperial
Majesty have desired a direct answer, I shall give such
an one as shall have neither horns nor teeth, viz., except
I be convinced with clear and undoubted evidence of
Holy Scripture—for I believe neither in the Pope nor
in councils alone, since it is evident they have often
erred and contradicted themselves—and as my conscience
is bound by God's Word, I cannot and will not recant,
because it is neither safe nor advisable to act contrary to
conscience. Here I stand ; I cannot do otherwise ; God
help me ! Amen !"

At about eight o'clock in the evening the diet adjourned. Darkness had set in, and the hall was dimly
lighted by torches. The assembly broke up with a feeling of excitement, which increased when Luther was
led away amid the hissing of the Spaniards. It was
generally believed that he would now be held as pris-

oner. Whilst he was standing in the midst of the throng, Duke Erich of Brunswick sent him a silver tankard of Eimbeck beer, with the message that he should drink and be refreshed. Luther enjoyed it right well, and said, "As Duke Erich has remembered me, so may our Lord Jesus Christ remember him in his last hour." Luther was now happy at heart. As soon as he returned to his lodging-place, he lifted up both hands and cried out, "I have done it; I have done it!" And continuing, he remarked : "If I had a thousand heads, I would lose them all rather than to recant."

The Elector was astonished at Luther's course. In the evening he said to Spalatin : "Well indeed has our father, Dr. Martin Luther, spoken in the presence of the Emperor and all the princes, both in Latin and German ; but he is too bold for me." The Emperor himself seems to have been very slightly impressed by the Augustinian monk. When, however, he spoke those memorable words, "Here I stand ; I cannot do otherwise," the Emperor was touched, and remarked, "The monk speaks without fear and with great courage." The day before he said, "This monk will never make a heretic of me."

The Emperor Charles possessed a very inadequate understanding of German affairs ; his knowledge of the German language was imperfect. He was a Spaniard at heart, and by his early education firmly attached to the doctrines of the Church. The new teachings of Luther, and the movement emanating therefrom, he viewed exclusively from a political standpoint.

On the following day the Emperor announced to the assembled members of the diet that since Martin Luther was not inclined to recede a finger's-breadth from his errors, after the example of his predecessors, who had always been obedient to the Roman Church, he must protect the ancient faith and maintain the authority of the Pope.

He would therefore be obliged to prosecute Luther with ban and interdict, and in every other available way. Yet he would not violate his promise of safe-conduct, but permit him to return to his home.

Before Luther left Worms another attempt was made to heal the strife by a friendly interchange of opinions. Yet after two days spent in negotiations Luther sent this declaration to the Archbishop of Treves : " Most gracious sir, I cannot recede.   Let God do unto me as He will. ' If this council or this work be of men, it will come to naught. But if it be of God, ye cannot overthrow it.' And thus, if my cause is not of God, it will not last more than two or three years ; but if it be of God, it cannot be overthrown."   Then he added : " I entreat your Grace to secure for me from his Imperial Majesty permission to return home ; for this is the tenth day of my sojourn here, and nothing has been accomplished."

Within three hours Luther received a letter of safe-conduct, with instructions to return to Wittenberg within twenty-one days, and on the way to abstain from exciting the people either by preaching or by writing.

On the 26th of April Luther and the friends who had accompanied him to Worms departed for home.   He rode in the same wagon in which he had come.   The imperial herald, Caspar Sturm, went with him as far as Friedberg.*   Here Luther dismissed him with a letter to the Emperor, in which he returns thanks for the safe-conduct, and offers both to do and to suffer all things for the sake of his Majesty and the empire.   But one thing, how-

---

* Not far from Frankfort.

ever, he must reserve : the right to profess the Word of
God, free and untrammelled.

On the 30th of October he reached Hersfeld,* where
in spite of ban and interdict he was received by the abbot
with distinguished honors and very hospitably entertained.
Luther writes to Spalatin about his reception as follows :
"The abbot sent his chancellor and chamberlain to welcome me a mile (German) from town ; he himself received me with a great retinue near his castle and escorted me into the city.   At the gates I was greeted by the
chief magistrate.   In the monastery I was gloriously
entertained and lodged ; the following morning at five
o'clock I was urged to preach, though I declined.   The
next day the abbot accompanied us to the edge of the
woods and through his chancellor provided for us all a
farewell dinner at Berka."*

Luther then continued on his journey to Eisenach,
whence many came out to meet him.   Here he preached,
notwithstanding the imperial injunction.   A portion of
his companions now left him, to take the direct route for
home.

But Luther, with two companions, visited some of his
relatives near Möhra.   Here he lodged with his uncle
Heinz, and preached on the 4th of May under a linden
tree near the church.   From Möhra he had intended to go
through the woods to Gotha.   His relatives accompanied
him as far as the Castle Altenstein ; there they bade him
farewell.   The wagon now disappeared into the woods
along a by-road that leads up to the Rennstieg, the
main thoroughfare.   In the neighborhood of the ruins of
a chapel, where to-day a sparkling spring gushes forth,

* On the road between Frankfort and Cassel, and not far from
Fulda.

close to "Luther's beech-tree," a company of armed
men suddenly burst out of the woods. As soon as one of
Luther's companions, his brother monk, saw them, he
jumped out of the wagon and fled, without a word of
farewell.

The armed horsemen surrounded the wagon, commanded the driver to halt, and seized Luther. They
allowed his other companion and the driver to continue
on their journey. Then, throwing a cloak about Luther,
they mounted him upon a horse, and led him about the
woods until night set in. It was nearly midnight when
the heavy drawbridge of the Wartburg Castle, near
Eisenach, was lowered, and when across it rode a weary
traveller, to be received within its sheltering walls.

CHAPTER X.

The news of Luther's capture spread with great rapidity. Neither friend nor enemy knew what had become of him, whether he were dead or yet alive. Even the warder of the gate of the Wartburg Castle was under the impression that an unknown offender had been caught on the road and securely lodged.

"Is he yet alive, or have they assassinated him?" asks the famous painter Albrecht Dürer,* as he continues his daily memorandum, saying, "This I do not know; but if dead, then he has suffered for the sake of Christian truth, and because he has punished the unchristian papacy that resists the freedom of Christ with its grievous burdens and human enactments. O God, if Luther be dead, who will henceforth so clearly proclaim to us the Gospel! O God, what could he not have written during the next ten or twenty years? O all ye pious Christian people, assist me to lament the loss of this inspired man, and to pray God that he send us another illuminated man!"

Yet even the enemies of Luther could not rejoice.

---

* Albrecht or Albert Dürer was born in Nuremberg May 20th, 1471, and died there April 6th, 1528. As engraver and painter, he was one of the most remarkable men of his age. He embraced the doctrines of the Reformation, and in his last and grandest works, life-size figures of the apostles John and Peter, and Mark and Paul, he is said to have entreated his countrymen to stand fast in the new faith.

Now that he was believed to be dead it was seen how greatly the people honored him, and how deep an impression his teachings had already produced. One of his enemies wrote to the Archbishop of Mayence (Mainz): "We have gotten rid of Luther, as we desired; but the people are so much excited about it that I fear we shall scarce escape with our lives, if we do not everywhere seek him with lanterns and call him back again."

In the meanwhile, in the month of May, the imperial edict against Luther had been proclaimed. In this he is declared to be cut off from the Church of God, as a hardened schismatic and a notorious heretic. Under penalty of punishment for high treason, and of the imperial ban and outlawry, it was forbidden to harbor and lodge, to entertain and nourish him, or to afford him help or support, secretly or openly, in word or deed, in any way whatsoever; but on the contrary, to seize him wherever found, and to deliver him to his Imperial Majesty. "No one shall buy or sell, read or retain his books; but they shall be blotted out of the memory of man."

In so severe and violent a manner did the Edict of Worms proceed against Luther, but without accomplishing anything. No one seemed to pay the least attention to it, and it was soon discovered that nothing would be gained even if Luther were removed.

During this time, Luther was securely lodged in the old burg of the Landgraves, which in his letters he called his Patmos (Rev. 1: 9), at times his mountain and desert, also his air-castle and home of the birds. He appeared to the inmates as a new knight, under the name of Squire George. He permitted his hair and beard to grow so that his personal appearance was changed. "You would hardly recognize me," he writes to Spalatin, "for I scarcely recognize myself."

Thus the plan of the Elector Frederick, to conceal Luther for a season and to secure him against persecutions, had well succeeded. Long before its execution the Elector had conceived of this idea, and at Worms he reached a final decision. Spalatin furnishes the following particulars of the event : "My gracious Lord, the Elector, was as yet somewhat faint-hearted, but he loved Martin Luther. He would not act contrary to God's Word, nor would he incur the enmity of the Emperor. And so he conceived the project of retiring Dr. Martin for a little while in hope that the controversy might quietly and peaceably be settled. Hence Luther was informed, on the evening previous to his departure from Worms, of the plan of seizing him, and expressed himself as contented to honor the Elector by humble obedience, although he would rather have gone straight forward without concealment." The commandant of the Wartburg Castle, Hans von Berlepsch, assisted by his friends Burkhard Hund von Wenkheim and Von Altenstein, admirably conducted and successfully executed the seizure and imprisonment of Luther.

The commander of the castle faithfully provided for him. Two pages of honor were in attendance. Whenever he left the burg a trusty and discreet knight accompanied him, and when disposed at any inn to lay aside his sword and to take up his books, to admonish him. On one occasion he joined a hunting party, but took no pleasure in the sport. "I have been on a hunt," he writes to Spalatin, "for the past two days, and have tasted of that bitter-sweet enjoyment of our noble lords ! We got two rabbits and a couple of poor partridges. A worthy occupation, in truth, for idle people ! I continued my theological studies amid the snares and the dogs ; and as much pleasure as I derived from viewing

such sport, the more sympathy and sorrow I had in thinking of the mysterious truth the picture concealed. For
the picture teaches nothing else than that the devil,
through his godless masters and dogs—the bishops and
theologians—secretly hunts and catches the innocent little
animals—the common people. It is the picture of simple
and believing souls which is thus vividly presented to my
sorrowing heart. And once it happened that a poor
little rabbit took refuge in the sleeve of my coat lying by
the way. The dogs in their pursuit scented its hiding-
place, first wounded, and then killed it. Thus the Pope
and Satan rage in their efforts to ruin saved souls, without
concerning themselves about my labors.''

He delighted to roam about the beautiful woods surrounding the castle searching for strawberries. This pas-
time was conducive to his health, for as late as October
of that year (1521) his bodily ailments caused him so much
trouble that he at one time intended to leave his asylum
and visit Erfurt for medical advice. He passed many a
day in melancholy and depression of spirits. At such
times he believed himself to be tormented by the Evil One.
Thus he relates the following incident : '' It was in the
year 1521 that I was in Patmos on the Wartburg, alone
in my little room, no one being permitted to come to me
save two pages of honor who brought me food and drink.
They had bought me a bag of hazelnuts, of which I ate
from time to time, and which I locked up in a chest.
One evening on retiring, I heard some one at the hazelnuts, cracking one after another with force against the
rafters ; then the noise approached my bed, but I cared
little for that. After I had fallen asleep there began
such a tumult on the stairway, as if threescore barrels
were being thrown down. I arose, went to the stairs,
and cried out, ' Art thou here ? (meaning the Evil One).

So be it!' I then commended my soul to the Lord Jesus Christ, of whom it is said (Psalm viii. 6), ' Thou hast put all things under His feet,' and retired to rest. For this is the best method to expel him (the devil): despising him and calling upon Christ. That he cannot endure." But finally, when Satan exceeded all bounds, as the legend records, Luther threw his inkstand at him, and he never returned again ! *

But neither sickness nor interdict could bend his will or paralyze his working powers. Not long had he been on the burg when he occupied himself with the translation of the Scriptures, as well as with other writings. In a few weeks several works were ready for the press. A treatise "About Confession, and whether the Pope is entitled to command the same," he dedicated to his particular friend and firm patron, Francisco von Sickingen.

Besides commenting upon selected portions of Holy Scripture intended to instruct, comfort, and edify Christian people, Luther sent out many a heavy controversial article from the Wartburg. Thus he directed a vigorous attack upon the Archbishop Albert of Mayence, brother of the Elector of Brandenburg. This Church dignitary, in need of money, had again set up the traffic with indulgences in the city of Halle, establishing a great shrine of relics, and inviting all to visit the same. He had collected a multitude of glorious relics, about nine thousand in number. Among these were remains of saints, a portion of the body of the patriarch Isaac, remnants of manna, pieces of Moses' burning bush, jugs

* The spot is still shown, in the Luther room of the Wartburg Castle, where the inkstand struck the wall. The plastering, however, has disappeared, being dug out and carried off by vandal visitors.

from the marriage feast at Cana, some of the wine
which Christ made of water on that occasion, thorns
from Jesus' martyr crown, one of the stones with which
Stephen was killed, and many other glorious relics.
Against all this abomination Luther wrote a treatise
entitled, "Against the Idol in Halle," and sent it to
Wittenberg for publication. The Elector Frederick,
however, did not favor Luther's attack upon one of the
foremost imperial princes, since such a step might pro-
voke a serious conflict and endanger the peace of the
Empire. Spalatin informed him of this, to which Luther
replied as follows: "I have hardly ever read a more
disagreeable letter than your last. First of all, I cannot
endure to hear it, that the Elector will not permit my
writing against that man of Mayence, nor anything that
will disturb the public peace. And yet, if I have with-
stood the Pope, wherefore should I retreat before his
creature?" But a little later on Luther listened to the
advice of his friends, and consented that the publication
of the treatise should be postponed. Then he sent a
written warning to the Archbishop, admonishing him
that if the traffic in indulgences were not immediately
stopped he would proclaim it to the whole world. He
would grant him two weeks' time for a proper answer.
After that he would issue his book, "Against the Idol
in Halle." Luther received the desired answer, a clear
evidence what a mighty power the concealed monk had
already developed against the Elector and the Archbishop
and Cardinal in Mayence. In his reply the Archbishop
said that the cause which led to Luther's treatise was
removed. He did not deny that he was a poor, sinful
man. He could endure Christian admonition, and hoped
to receive grace and strength of God to live according
to His will. Luther put but little faith in the statements

of the Archbishop, although he desisted from publishing his treatise.

Above all other writings Luther delighted to work upon his German Church Postils, an explanation of the Gospels and Epistles for Sundays and festival days, which was the first collection of sermons in the German language.

But the finest and ripest fruit of Luther's leisure and seclusion from the world was his translation of the New Testament. It is the principal work and the crown of all his Wartburg labors. He comments upon it as follows : "I will remain here in seclusion until Eastertide. In the meanwhile I will write the Church Postils, and intend to translate the New Testament into the German tongue, as many of my friends request. O that every city had its interpreter, and that all tongues, hands, eyes, ears, and hearts might concern and busy themselves about this one book ! I will translate the Bible, although in so doing I have assumed a task which will exceed my powers. I now perceive what it is to translate, and why up to the present time it has never been undertaken by any one who has subscribed his name. But the Old Testament I will not touch, unless you (meaning the professors and friends at Wittenberg) will assist me. Indeed, if I could have a secret room at Wittenberg I would go there at once, and with your assistance translate the whole of it from the beginning. But I would have such a translation as would deserve to be read by all Christians, for I hope we would be able to present to Germany a better translation than is the Latin version. It is a great work, and worthy of our united labors, since it ought everywhere to be found and to conduce to the general welfare of the people." In two months Luther had completed the translation

of the New Testament. "I translated not only St.
John's Gospel," says Luther, "but the entire New
Testament, whilst I was in Patmos.   And now Philip
(Melanchthon) and I have begun to polish it off, and
with God's help it will be a fine piece of work.   For my
fellow-Germans was I born, and them will I serve!''
And in order that he might do this right well, he ques-
tioned the mother at home, the children in the streets,
and the common laborer in the market.   The terms of
court and palace he could not use, said he.   And thus
he accomplished the completion of a truly popular,
glorious work, which proved to be the foundation and
corner-stone of his Reformation labors.

CHAPTER XI.

"O WOULD that I were in Wittenberg!" sighed Luther, as he was seated at his study-table in his lonely room on the Wartburg. Unrest and longing drew him back to his old circle and sphere of activity at Wittenberg.

In the meanwhile his friends had quietly and faithfully continued the work. They were resigned to the necessary absence of their master when Melanchthon joyfully announced to them, "Our dearest Father still lives." And Luther, in his seclusion, rejoiced to hear of the effective labors of his colleagues, through whose influence the university was visibly prospering. From all parts of Germany, Switzerland, Poland, and from other lands, young men flocked together and labored with zeal and in perfect harmony. A beginning was made to carry out in practice that for which Luther had contended in word. To bring the Church life in accord with the new doctrines was the question of the day.

Luther himself assisted in its solution with counsel and consolation. He was painfully aware of his personal responsibility in the matter, for he acknowledged that it was he who had first lighted the fires. He also felt that he was under special obligations to the congregation at Wittenberg as its teacher and spiritual shepherd. And indeed his counsel was necessary. For a great excitement had arisen, and the strain upon the public mind was daily growing more intense. It happened on this wise.

The first step to be taken in the practical reform movement was to abolish the system of monasticism, and to
change the administration of the Lord's Supper so as
to conform to the institution of Christ. To this end
Karlstadt, one of Luther's colleagues, labored with great
zeal. But his restless spirit was not content with the
slow devolopment of things. He appeared as a fiery
preacher, and, notwithstanding his weak voice and un-
gainly appearance, he attracted a multitude of hearers.
After he had drawn around him a large number of followers, he forcibly entered the castle church one day, drove
out the priests that were reading mass, and began a furious
destruction of pictures, statues, and altars. He also desired to establish a law making marriage obligatory upon
the clergy, and allowing none but married men to be
called to Church offices. He proposed to the Elector
that private masses should be abolished on his territory.
He exhorted monks and nuns to leave their cloisters. The
Lord's Supper was to be celebrated according to its
original institution, and moreover so that twelve com-
municants at a time should receive the bread and the
wine together. Melanchthon, mild and yielding in his
disposition, could not withstand these stormy and violent
proceedings. He wrote to Luther that he had entreated
Karlstadt to moderate his zeal, but that he alone could
not stem the current.

Thereupon Luther, in the attire of a knight, and ac-
companied by a single servant, secretly returned to
Wittenberg. For three days he lodged with his friend
Amsdorf,* none but his most intimate associates knowing

---

* Nicholas von Amsdorf was born Dec. 3d, 1483, and died May
14th, 1565. He was one of the most energetic, and at times most
violent, of Luther's adherents.

aught of his arrival. After he had comforted his friends and strengthened them by his counsels for their work, he again secretly returned to the Wartburg.

The Elector was not yet willing that Luther should leave his place of refuge. Nor was his presence in Wittenberg absolutely necessary, although scenes of disorder had occurred, and priests and monks had been abused by students and townspeople.

In Zwickau * numerous disturbances, especially as touching infant baptism, had occurred. Three of the prime movers came to Wittenberg during the Christmas holidays in the year 1521. They were curious fellows in warlike attire. Wonderful experiences did they relate : God had conversed with them ; they could foretell future events ; in short, they claimed to be prophets and apostles ! Melanchthon thought that they were possessed of a particular spirit, whatever be its nature, and that Luther alone could determine its true character. But Luther did not wish to return on that account, especially since it was not the desire of the Elector. He wrote to Melanchthon, and also to his friend Amsdorf, that the prophets of Zwickau should not be heard at once, but that the matter should quietly take its course. An investigation of their claims to a special calling should be held, and their spirits should be tried according to the advice of St. John (I. 4 : 1), whether they be of God. To Luther it looked very suspicious that they should boast of their intimate conversations with God. To the people of Wittenberg Luther wrote a letter reproving them for having

* Zwickau, a city of Saxony, about sixty miles south-west of Dresden, has a present population of about 30,000. Thomas Münzer, one of the leaders of the Anabaptist disturbances, was pastor here in 1520. The town suffered severely during the Thirty Years' War, its population being reduced from 10,000 to less than 5000.

introduced innovations in connection with the mass, for destroying pictures, etc., all of which were matters of no great consequence, and which faith and love could tolerate.

But when Melanchthon and his friends saw that they could not stem the current alone, they continued to entreat Luther to return. He only could bring help and deliverance. None but he could lead the devastating stream back again into its proper course. Luther finally yielded to these entreaties, though the Elector would not listen to such a proposal. He commanded him to remain on the Wartburg, since in Wittenberg he could not afford him protection. For in the event of his return to the university, Duke George of Saxony in his wrath would demand the immediate execution of the imperial edict. But Luther could no longer be detained. He was impelled to return to his congregation at Wittenberg and with a firm hand to lead the Reformation movement back to its proper channel, and henceforth to guide it in his own spirit.

CHAPTER XII.

ON the 1st of March, 1522, Luther left his cherished refuge which had so securely protected him. From his stopping-place at Borna, near Leipsic, on the second day of his journey from the Wartburg to Wittenberg, he informed the Elector, by letter, of his departure from the castle. This communication, which is a remarkable memorial of faith, reads as follows :

" *Most August and Honorable Elector and Gracious Sire!*

" The gracious letter of Your Highness reached me on Friday evening previously to my departure on the following morning. That you wrote with the very best of intentions toward me, needs neither proof nor testimony, for I honor myself by this conviction, so far as human knowledge goes.

" But for my part I would say, that your Lordship may know, or you may not know—hence be it known unto you—that I have received the Gospel not from men, but from Heaven alone, through our Lord Jesus Christ. Therefore I would be entitled to subscribe myself a servant and an evangelist, as indeed I propose to do henceforth. And that I exposed myself to trial and judgment was not because I doubted the truth, but because of an abundance of humility to attract others to the same. I have done enough for you, in that I vacated my position during the past year, to obey Your Grace. For the devil knows full well that I did it not for fear. He knew my heart when I arrived at Worms ; for had I known that as many devils were lying in wait for me as there were tiles on the houses, I would nevertheless have joyfully leaped in among them.

"But now Duke George is not even equivalent to a single devil ! And since the Father of unfathomable mercies hath made us to be lords over death and all devils— and since he hath given unto us the wealth of assurance that we may say unto him, ' Abba, Father,' you may well judge that it would be the highest reproach unto such a Father, did we not believe that we are also lords over Duke George's wrath. As to myself, I am persuaded, that I would enter into his city, Leipsic—pardon what may seem foolish to you—should it rain nothing but Duke Georges for nine days, and if each one of them were nine times more wrathful than this one. He seems to regard my Lord Jesus Christ as a man of straw, which reproach He, my Lord, and I can suffer for a while. But I will not conceal from you the fact that I have often prayed for and mourned over Duke George, that God might enlighten him. I will once more weep and pray for him, and then never more. And I entreat you also to help and pray that we turn the evil away from him, that—O Lord God !—is controlling him without respite. I would quickly slay Duke George with a single word if any good would come of it.

"I have written this with the intent that you may know that I am going to Wittenberg under much higher protection than that of the Elector. Nor is it my purpose to ask protection of the latter. On the contrary, I am inclined to think that I can protect the Elector more and better than he can me. Indeed, if I knew that you could and would protect me I would not go to Wittenberg. No sword can help this cause of mine. God alone can help, without any human co-operation. Therefore, he that has the most faith will be able to afford the most protection. And since I perceive that you are yet weak in the faith, I cannot regard you to be the man who can either protect or save me.

"And since you desire to know what assistance you can render at this time, and are of the opinion that you have done too little, I answer most obediently, that you have already done too much, and that you ought to do nothing more. For God cannot and will not endure our worrying and striving. He will have it all left unto Him, and unto none other. Govern yourself accordingly.

"If you believe this, you will be safe and enjoy peace. But if you do not believe this, then will I believe it, and must see your unbelief torment you with cares, an experience which all unbelievers righteously suffer. And now, since I do not intend to obey your commands, you are blameless before God, whether I am imprisoned or killed. But over against man you are thus to conduct yourself : as Elector you are to be obedient to the superior authority, and suffer His Imperial Majesty to rule in city and country, according to the laws of the empire. You are not to defend me, or to resist or to interpose any hindrance whatsoever against the power that is seeking to capture or to kill me. For no one is entitled to resist the powers that be save He who ordained the same ; otherwise it would be rebellion, and against God. Yet I hope you will be controlled by reason, and recognize the fact that you were born of too noble ancestry to become my jailer yourself.

"If you will leave the gate open and assure me of your safe-conduct, in case my enemies or their represen-

tatives should come to fetch me, you will have rendered
sufficient obedience.　They cannot demand of you more
than this, to ascertain Luther's abiding-place.　And that
they may know without care, or work, or danger, on your
part.　For Christ hath not taught me to be a Christian
to the injury of others.　But should they be so unreason-
able as to command you to seize me, then I will declare
what shall be done.　I will secure you, as touching my
cause, against danger to body and soul and possessions ;
you may believe this, or you may not.

"Herewith I commend you to the grace of God.　As
to other matters, we shall consider them when it becomes
necessary.　I have hurriedly finished this letter in order
that you may not feel disturbed by the reports of my arrival ; for I must be of comfort and not of injury to
every man, if I would be a true Christian.　I am now
treating with a different man from Duke George ; he
knows me right well, and I am also tolerably acquainted
with him.　If you had faith you would see the glory of
God !　But since you have not believed, you have as yet
seen nothing.　May God be loved and praised in all
eternity !　Amen.

"Given at Borna, on Ash Wednesday, A.D. 1522.

"Your Grace's * obedient servant,

"MARTIN LUTHER."

The course of Luther's journey led him through Jena.
Here, at the " Inn of the Black Bear," he met two Swiss
students who were on their way to the University of Wit-

---

* The repetition of the titles " Your Grace," etc., which occur
very frequently throughout the letter, is omitted in the above
translation.　They add nothing to the meaning, but serve to moderate the boldness of the spirit in which the epistle is written.

tenberg. One of them, John Kessler * of St. Gall, who afterward figured as a reformer in his native country, has preserved a very pleasing account of their meeting with Luther. His narrative has come down to us, and begins as follows : " While on our journey to Wittenberg, for the purpose of studying the Holy Scriptures, we arrived at Jena, in Thuringia. We sought about town for an inn where we could lodge for the night, but we were everywhere refused ; for it was Shrove Tuesday (Fastnacht, carnival night), when not much attention is paid to strangers and pilgrims. We were about leaving the city to seek lodgings in a neighboring village, when we were met at the gates by an honorable gentleman, who addressed us in a friendly manner and desired to know whither we were bound at so late an hour of the day."

After the two students had informed him of their dilemma he showed them the Inn of the Black Bear, where they obtained lodgment for the night.

Then Kessler continues the story : " In the waiting-room of the inn we found a man seated alone at a table poring over a little book that lay open before him. He greeted us kindly, and asked us to be seated at his table [on account of their travel-stained clothing they had seated themselves to one side, on a bench near the

---

* John Jacob Kessler was born at St. Gall in Switzerland in the year 1502. He prepared himself for the priesthood at Basel, and continued his studies at Wittenberg. On his return to his native city he renounced his intentions to become a priest, but as a layman rendered good service to the cause of the Reformation. He finally consented to be ordained, at the age of forty, as Protestant minister, and thereafter took a prominent part in developing the interests of church and school in his canton. He died in 1574, aged seventy-two years.

door]. Then he offered us drink, which we could not well refuse. After thus perceiving his friendliness and cordiality, we joined him at his table and ordered some wine, that we might offer to him in return. We took him to be a knight, who, according to the custom of the country, was clad in pants and doublet, without armor, with a little red leather cap on his head, a short sword at his side, his right hand resting on the hilt, the left hand grasping the manuscript. His eyes were black and deep-set, lightening and sparkling like the stars, so that one could hardly look at them for any length of time.

"Soon he began to ask us where we were born, but answered the question himself by saying, 'You are natives of Switzerland, and of what part?'

"We answered, 'Of St. Gall.'

"Then he remarked, 'If you intend to go to Wittenberg you will find excellent fellow-countrymen there— Jerome Schurf and his brother Doctor Augustine Schurf.'

"'We have letters of introduction to these gentlemen,' said we; and then asked him, 'Sir, can you tell us whether Martin Luther is again at Wittenberg, or if not there where he may be?'

"'I have been reliably informed,' was the stranger's answer, 'that Luther is not in Wittenberg at the present time, but he will soon be there. Philip Melanchthon is there, and teaches the Greek language, and there are others that teach Hebrew. Confidentially, I would advise you to study both Greek and Hebrew, for they are both necessary to understand the Scriptures.'"

The two students declared that they would not rest content until they had seen and heard the man who had attacked priestcraft and the mass. "'We, too, have been preparing for the ministerial office, at the wish of our parents, and we should like very much to know all about these things.'

" ' Where have you studied ? ' asked the stranger.

" ' In Basel,' we replied.

" ' Well, what is the outlook in Basel ? ' continued he. ' Is Erasmus still there, and how fares it with him ? '

" ' As far as we know, matters are progressing right well in Basel,' we answered. ' Erasmus is still there, but what he is doing is unknown to every one, for he is very quiet and uncommunicative.'

" ' But what think they of that man Luther in Switzerland ? '

" ' There are, as elsewhere, various opinions entertained concerning him. Some cannot find words enough to praise him, and to thank God that He revealed His truth through him and uncovered error. Others condemn him as an insufferable heretic—especially the clergy.'

" ' Methinks these are the priests,' remarked the stranger."

Soon the strange knight became very intimate with the two students. His learned conversation, especially his acquaintance with the Schurf brothers, with Melanchthon and Erasmus, were both surprising and wonderful to them. And their astonishment was still further increased when one of them opened the book that lay upon the table and found it to be a Hebrew Psalter. He replaced it, and the stranger took it up.

"I would willingly lose one of my fingers," said one of the students, "if I could understand that language."

"You may readily acquire it," replied the unknown one, "if you will apply yourself with diligence. I, too, desire to make progress with it, and daily exercise myself in it."

The day had now fairly ended, and thick darkness had

set in.   The proprietor of the inn had entered the room and approached the table at which Luther and the two Swiss students were seated.   When he observed their ardent desire to learn of the whereabouts of Luther, he remarked, "My dear fellows, had you been here two days ago you would have seen him, for he was seated at this table and in this very place," pointing with his finger to the seat.   "We were chagrined at this," continues Kessler in his narrative, "and were angry with ourselves that we had dallied by the way; we blamed the muddy and rough roads that impeded our progress, and then said, 'Nevertheless, we rejoice that we are in the same house and at the same table where he was.'   At this the host laughed and walked away."

"After a little while the innkeeper called me out of the room," continues Kessler.   "I was frightened and bethought myself of what I had done or was suspected of. But the host said to me, 'Since you so ardently desire to see and hear Luther, know then that it is he that is sitting with you at table.'   I was inclined to think that he was imposing upon me, and so I said, 'You would like, no doubt, to fool me, and to satisfy my desires with a counterfeit of Luther.'   But he assured me that he was speaking the truth, yet entreated me to act as if I were not aware of it.   I returned to the waiting-room, but could not refrain from whispering into the ear of my companion, 'The host tells me that this man is Luther.' But he would not believe it, and replied, 'You have misunderstood him; perhaps he said it was Hutten. And now since his apparel reminded me more of Hutten than of Luther—for Luther was a monk—I was persuaded to believe that the innkeeper said, 'It is Hutten,' for the first syllables of the two names, Luther and Hutten, resemble each other.' "

In the meanwhile two merchants entered the inn, and after they had laid aside their wrappings, one of them placed an unbound book upon the table. The unknown knight asked them for the name and nature of the book. "It is Dr. Luther's Explanation of the Gospels and Epistles, recently printed and published; have you not yet seen it?" remarked one of the traders. "I shall soon receive a copy of the work," replied the stranger. Just then the host approached and invited them all to supper. "But we requested him," says Kessler, "to allow us to eat by ourselves, evidently not feeling able to pay for a full meal. 'My dear fellows,' said the innkeeper, 'I will provide for you according to your means; come and be seated.' When the stranger heard these remarks, he added, 'Come and eat; I will settle the bill with our host.'

"Whilst at table his conversation was so friendly and blessed that we paid more attention to his words than to our victuals. He spoke of the impending imperial diet at Nuremberg, but did not think much would come of it, since the noble lords would rather spend their time upon expensive tournaments, sleighing parties, and idle display, than hear the Word of God. 'But I hope,' said he, 'that the pure truth and God's Word will bring more fruit among our children and posterity than it does among their parents, in whom error is so deeply rooted that it cannot be removed.'

"The merchants also expressed their opinion, the older one of the two saying, 'I am a simple-minded, straightforward layman, and do not understand much about these quarrels. But as the thing appears to me, Luther is either an angel out of heaven or a devil out of hell. I would willingly spend ten florins here, for his sake, if I could confess unto him, persuaded, as I am, that he could and would well enlighten my conscience.'

"In the meanwhile the host drew near to us and quietly whispered, 'Do not be concerned about the payment of the meal; Martinus (meaning Luther) has arranged for that.' At this we were much rejoiced, not because of the money, nor because of the enjoyment of the meal, but because this man had treated us as his guests. After the supper the merchants left the inn to attend to their horses, leaving us alone with the unknown one in the waiting-room. We thanked him for the evening meal, and gave him to understand that we took him to be Ulrich von Hutten.

"'I am not the man,' he replied; and to the inn-keeper, who at that moment entered the room, he remarked, 'I have been created a nobleman this evening, for these Swiss students take me to be Ulrich von Hutten.'

"'You are not he,' replied the host, 'but you are Martin Luther.' At this he laughed in high glee, saying, 'These take me to be Hutten; you regard me as Luther; soon I shall be called Martinus Marcolfus.'

"Thereupon he invited us to drink with him a friendly and parting blessing. And as I was about taking a glass of beer he proffered me a glass of wine, saying, 'You are unaccustomed to beer, drink the wine.'

"Then he arose, and throwing his tabard over his shoulders he took leave of us, grasping us by the hand and saying, 'When you reach Wittenberg present my greeting to Doctor Jerome Schurf.'

"'We shall willingly do so,' we replied, 'but from whom shall we say does the greeting come?' Whereupon he concluded:

"'Tell him simply this: He that cometh, sends his

greeting.' With this final word he parted from us and retired to rest."

The merchants, returning to the room, resumed their social intercourse, and continued their inquiries concerning the unknown guest. The innkeeper still held him to be Luther, and the merchants at length were persuaded to believe him ; but they were worried about their awkward remarks in his presence. They concluded to arise betimes, and to beg his pardon ; and this they did.

They found him in the stable early in the morning, presented their apology, and received the following reply : " You said last evening that you were willing to spend ten florins on Luther's account to be permitted to confess to him ; if you should ever confess to him, then you will see and know whether or not I am Martin Luther." With this he mounted his horse and rode toward Wittenberg.

" Upon our arrival in Wittenberg we presented our letters of introduction to Dr. Jerome Schurf. And when we entered the reception room we beheld Martin Luther, the same man whom we had seen in the inn at Jena. And in his company were Philip Melanchthon,* Justus Jonas, Nicholas Amsdorf, and Doctor Augustine Schurf, recounting to him the events which had transpired in Wittenberg during his absence from the university. Luther

---

* Philip Melanchthon has been aptly termed the second leader of the Protestant Reformation. He was born at Bretten, in Baden, in 1497, and died at Wittenberg in 1560. His family name was Schwarzerd (black earth), but his uncle, the famous Reuchlin, translated it into Greek, and hence Melanchthon. He was pre-eminently the scholar and theologian as Luther was the hero and the advocate of the Reform movement. Modest, gentle, and peaceful, he supplemented Luther's fiery zeal and determined will. To the end of his life his fervent prayer was for the unity of Christian believers.

greeted us, and, smiling, pointed at Philip Melanchthon and said : ' This is he of whom I spake unto you.' The latter then conversed with us, inquiring about many things, upon which we informed him to the best of our knowledge. And thus we passed the day with these men, to our great delight."

CHAPTER XIII.

AFTER Luther returned to Wittenberg the excitement soon subsided, and order was restored. With a firm and steady hand he laid hold upon the control of affairs. He again made his residence in the monastery, and exchanged his knight's attire for the monk's cowl, which he did not finally lay aside until two years thereafter. For eight days in succession he preached against the disturbers of the peace with marked power and great success. He exhorted all to maintain love and concord, and that believing Christians should treat one another, as God had treated them, in love, which love they enjoyed by faith. He pointed out the difference between things necessary and things permissible, and instructed his hearers upon the administration of the Lord's Supper and upon Confession. And thus in a short time the storm was allayed.

He did not spend much time upon the prophets of Zwickau. He allowed them to present their cause, and then said that nothing which they had offered was founded upon the Holy Scriptures, and that their views were but the pernicious suggestions of a deceitful spirit and the imagination of inquisitive dispositions. "I have also detected them in obvious falsehoods," writes Luther. "And when they endeavored to evade my statements with miserably smooth words, I commanded them to substantiate their teachings with miracles, of which they

boasted even against Scripture. They refused to do so
but threatened that I would yet be obliged to believ
them. Thereupon I·charged their god not to perforn
any miracles against the will of my God, and thus w
separated." On the same day they left Wittenberg, an
afterward sent a letter to Luther full of reviling an
imprecation.

After peace and order had been restored in Wittenberg
upon invitation of John,* brother of the Elector Frederick
Luther proclaimed his doctrines in Zwickau, Borna
Erfurt, and Weimar. He resumed the delivery of h
university lectures, and also devoted himself to literar
labors and controversial writings. He entered upon
severe conflict with Henry VIII., King of England, wh
in reply to Luther's treatise about the Babylonian Cap
tivity had written a book entitled "Defence and Ad
ministration of the Seven Sacraments against Marti
Luther." For this he received from the Pope the hon
orary title of "Defender of the Faith."

In the course of the year (1522) there appeare
Luther's German version of the New Testament. It ha
been finished on the Wartburg, revised with the aid of
Melanchthon and issued from the press on the 21st of
September. Thousands eagerly called for it, in spite of
the high selling price, one and a half florins.† In n

---

* John the Constant was born in 1468, and died in 1532. H
was the personal friend and ardent supporter of Luther and th
Reformation. He succeeded his brother Frederick as Elector of
Saxony, in the year 1525.

† The florin was originally a silver coin of Florence, first coine
there in the twelfth century. The name was adopted in differen
European countries and applied to gold and silver coins varyin
in value, the single florin being worth from about 25 to 50 cent
Estimating the purchasing power of money then at double wha
it is now, a copy of Luther's Testament would have cost $1.50

other way was the gospel so generally diffused and the cause strengthened as through the Holy Scriptures, which could now be read by all classes of the people. The Roman Catholic Church recognized the danger, and immediately prohibited its circulation.

One of the most violent enemies of Luther writes as follows : " In a marvellous manner did the printers multiply the copies of Luther's New Testament, so that cobblers and women, and every layman acquainted with German letters, most eagerly read it as the source of truth, and by frequent reading impressed it upon their memory. Many indeed presumed to obtain so much knowledge within a few weeks that they ventured to dispute about the faith and the Gospel with masters and doctors of sacred Theology ; for Luther has long taught them that even Christian women are priests, and indeed that every one that is baptized is as much a priest as Pope, bishop, and presbyter. The great mass of Lutherans give themselves a great deal more trouble to learn the Scriptures thus translated than do the Catholic people, who let the priests and monks attend to that."

In the same year portions of the Old Testament, such as the five books of Moses, were finished and issued in parts. Additional portions were published in 1524. But the work of translating the prophets delayed the issue of the whole Bible for several years.

Leo X. was dead, and a new Pope, Adrian VI.,* had

---

* Pope Adrian VI. was born in 1459, became Pope in 1522, and died in 1523. He is said to have been the son of an obscure mechanic of Utrecht, named Boeijens. The simplicity of his court, his attempted ecclesiastical reforms, and his humble acknowledgment of errors in the Church gave great offence to the clergy. In one of his published works he held that a Pope might err even in matters of faith.

ascended the papal throne. Earnest and severe in disposition, he sought most emphatically to crush Luther's
heresy, which, in spite of ban and edict, was making con-
tinual progress. Nor did he hesitate to attack Luther's
personal character, and to heap abuse upon him. Luther
was not disturbed at this; he was accustomed to call
Adrian "the jackass!" At the meeting of the Imperial
diet in Nuremberg (1522) Adrian met with no favor.
He was plainly told that the numerous abuses of the papal
court and of the Roman clergy, by means of which the
German people were insufferably burdened, were the
main causes why the Pope's decrees and Emperor's edicts
against Luther could not be enforced. At the same time
a free council of the universal Christian Church was demanded.

The Pope now addressed a violent communication to
the Elector, abounding in serious threats. "Did I but
know of a way," writes Luther, "how to deliver the Elector out of all this difficulty, without reproach to the Gospel,
I would not spare my life. One year ago I anticipated
losing my life for the cause, and I thought that this
might be the way of deliverance for him. But now, since
we are not able to fathom and comprehend God's plans, we
shall rest in safety when we say : Thy will be done. And
I doubt not that the Elector will escape unharmed so
long as he does not openly confess and approve of my
cause. But God alone knows why he must bear my
shame. This much, however, is certain, that it will do
him no harm ; on the contrary, it will be his greatest
blessing." The next Imperial Diet, held in 1534, likewise refused to proceed against Luther, as demanded by
the new Pope, Clement VII., a counterpart of Leo X.
But the Elector entertained the hope that all would yet
peacefully unite upon Luther's doctrine.

The influence of Luther's activity was everywhere felt. Many noblemen and a number of cities espoused his cause, and called Lutheran pastors. Among the former was Albert, Earl of Mansfeld. Among the latter, Magdeburg, Frankfort, Nuremberg, Ulm, Strasburg, Breslau, and Bremen. In Saxony Zwickau, Altenburg, and Eisenach headed the list. But the first country that, as a whole, accepted the evangelical teachings was Prussia, the land of the Teutonic Knights.* Albert of Brandenburg, the grand-master of the order, brother of the Elector of Brandenburg, corresponded with Luther, and also, through oral communication with him, became well grounded in the evangelical doctrines. He, together with two bishops, George von Polenz and Erhard von Queiss, accepted Luther's doctrine. The dominion of the order was converted into a civil government, and its grand-master became Duke of Prussia.

Thus there was erected in the north-eastern part of Germany a firm bulwark of Protestantism. But at the same time there arose violent and bloody persecutions of the Lutherans. The Emperor was not favorably disposed. In the Netherlands cruel punishments were inflicted, and elsewhere the zealots of Romanism were also active. The greater the number of adherents secured by the new doctrines, the sharper were the issues drawn and the more determined the opposition. Many that in the beginning

---

* The Teutonic Knights were a religious and military order which originated during the crusades. It acquired extensive landed possessions in the north-eastern part of Germany in the thirteenth and fourteenth centuries, and reached its greatest prosperity in the fifteenth century, when its territory extended from the River Oder to the Gulf of Finland. Internal dissensions, a spirit of luxury, and warfare with the Kings of Poland completed its downfall in the sixteenth century.

favored Luther's teachings, afterward withdrew their support, so firmly were they attached to old forms and usages. Thus, for example, Luther's old friend and spiritual adviser, John von Staupitz, retired to Salzburg. To him there was nothing at stake in the Reformation movement of so much importance that the peace and the unity of the Church should be endangered. This alienation and retirement of his paternal friend painfully affected Luther. But with equanimity he endured the attack of Erasmus,* who in the beginning had apparently supported him. He regarded him as a man possessed of a superficial, worldly mind, and blind to the highest truths of salvation.

But Luther was now less concerned about controversy than he was about the work of planting and building. His chief aim was to have the Word of God proclaimed in the congregations, so that the latter might be built up with faith and prayer, petition and thanksgiving. In this sense he proceeded to reform the order of service, excluding all unchristian additions. To make good this loss he endeavored to secure real German church chorals. He besought his friends to transpose the Psalms for this purpose, he himself setting the example. In the year 1524 there appeared in Wittenberg the first German hymn-book, consisting of eight hymns, among them the one beginning, "Now, rejoice, ye Christian people." In the preface he remarks: "I am

---

* Erasmus was born in Rotterdam 1467, and died in Basel 1536. He was the foremost linguist of his times, and indirectly aided the Reformation as a scholar rather than as a thinker. He pursued a middle course, agreeable to neither party—in favor of reforming the vices of the clergy, but opposed to doctrinal changes or reforms. He was timid in disposition and compromising in character.

not of the opinion that all the arts should be suppressed by the Gospel, and should perish, as several high ecclesiastics maintain ; but I would rather that all the arts, especially music, should be enlisted in the service of Him who has created them and bestowed them upon us.'' And he was forced to view with deep regret the arts and sciences endangered by those intemperate fanatics, who, in their false zeal, would have destroyed all the external decoration of the churches.

He also greatly emphasized the need of the correct training and the proper instruction of the young. He published a treatise in 1524, entitled, '' To the Councillors of all the cities in Germany, to establish and maintain Christian Schools.'' And thus there went out from him an influence which has had the most powerful, glorious, and far-reaching effect. Luther was not only the renewer of the religious life of the German people, but he was also the father and creator of its common schools, that gigantic tree whose branches have spread over all Germany—and it may fairly be said over all Protestantism—scattering blessings over all classes of society, to the glory of God and the welfare of mankind.

CHAPTER XIV.

BUT a new danger threatened the cause of the Reformation. It did not proceed from its outward foes, nor even from the imperial or papal powers, but from its own adherents. "All my enemies heretofore," writes Luther, "as hard as some have pressed me, have not hurt me as much as have some of our own people."

But above all others did Karlstadt's* behavior occasion him care and sorrow. Upon Luther's return from the Wartburg, Karlstadt openly maintained peace and order, but secretly favored the fanatics of Zwickau. The parish of Orlamünde, a dependency of Wittenberg, becoming vacant, Karlstadt took possession in his own name and right, and began to introduce reforms. Pictures and crucifixes were removed from the church and destroyed. He taught his own views, and carried out his own practices relative to the Lord's Supper, and endeavored to enforce many Old Testament teachings. Thus, he

---

* Andrew Rudolph Bodenstein was born in Karlstadt, Franconia, and, according to the custom of the times, he added the birthplace to his name, and was known by the former. He was somewhat older than Luther. He studied at Wittenberg, secured his academical degrees, and obtained a professorship in the same institution. After his expulsion from Germany he lived for a while at Strasburg and Zürich, and was subsequently appointed professor in the University of Basel, which position he held until his death in 1541.

forbade the paying and taking of interest on money loaned, and even went so far as to recommend the introduction of the system of polygamy as practised by the ancient Hebrews.

Spiritually related to Karlstadt was Thomas Münzer.* In the year 1523, about Easter-tide, he had managed to secure the parish of Allstedt. His object was to set up a kingdom of saints on earth, with external power and pomp. He proposed to destroy the godless and the tyrannical, appealing to the Word of the Old Testament, in which the chosen people of God were obliged to extirpate the heathen inhabitants of the promised land, to destroy their altars and burn their idols. And, like Karlstadt, he also preached communism. Whoever among the princes or nobles would not consent to this arrangement should be decapitated or hanged. His principal associate was the former monk, Pfeiffer of Mühlhausen. Münzer accused Luther of a free-and-easy, carnal life. The latter retorted, "Let them alone to preach what they will ; if any be led astray, it happens as in war, where there is conflict and battle, some will be wounded and fall." Antichrist must be destroyed without the sword. Christ contends with the Spirit. So thought Luther. But when he heard that Münzer and his followers intended to use force, he desired the authorities to intervene and to say, "Desist from the use of force ; the power is ours ; otherwise, leave the country."

At the request of the Elector, Luther undertook a journey, in the year 1524, to Weimar, Jena, and

---

* Thomas Münzer was born in 1490, at Stolberg, in the Harz Mountains. In early youth he developed an adventurous disposition, which clung to him until death.

Orlamünde.* At Weimar he wrote and sent a communication to the council and congregation at Mühlhausen,
warning them against Thomas Münzer. In Jena, where
he again lodged at the Inn of the Black Bear, he delivered a sermon directed against insurrection and icono-
clastic destruction. Here also he met Karlstadt, and
held a stormy interview with him. He accused him of
being in league with the fanatical "new prophets," and
demanded of him that he should openly write and preach
against them. Karlstadt complained, on the other
hand, that Luther had treated him too vehemently, and
that he had classified him with the rebellious and murderous spirits.

After this interview Luther continued on his journey,
by way of Kahla and Neustadt, to Orlamünde, head-
quarters of Karlstadt. But he accomplished nothing
here; he narrowly escaped bodily violence. He himself
narrates this experience: "When I reached Orlamünde
I soon discovered what kind of seed Karlstadt had sown;
for I was greeted with such a blessing as this: 'Depart in
the name of a thousand devils, and may you break your
neck before you leave the city!'"

Luther reported to the Elector on his return home.
As to Karlstadt, he wrote that he had completely gone
astray, and that there was but little hope of his restora-
tion. He thought that Karlstadt had always ignored
the praise of Christ, and that he would always do so.
"His own insane desire for fame and praise has brought
him to this. He has proved to be our most dangerous
enemy, so that I am inclined to believe the poor, miser-

* Orlamünde, Weimar, Jena, Kahla, Neustadt, Mühlhausen, and
Frankenhausen are all located in Thuringia. Mühlhausen has
recently again come into notice as being the birthplace of the elder
Roebling, the engineer of the Brooklyn Bridge.

able wretch is possessed of an evil spirit. God have mercy on his sins with which he is offending unto death.''

The Elector then determined that Karlstadt must leave the country. He complied with this order, going first to Strasburg, and thence to Basel. From the latter city he issued a number of pamphlets against Luther, in which he terms him a double papist and a friend of Antichrist. Luther replied with a pamphlet entitled, ''Against the Celestial Prophets.'' He warned against them because they taught without authority, and because they avoided and were silent upon the principal part of Christian doctrine, viz., how we should be delivered of our sins, obtain a good conscience, and a happy heart at peace with God. On the other hand, they frightened and deceived the conscience with new and curious teachings.

And in a short time the harvest of the seed which the false prophets had sown was fully ripe, and the storm broke with fury.

Münzer, after having preached insurrection in southwestern Germany, arrived in Mühlhausen. By means of his public addresses and specious promises he attracted and attached the people to himself. A parish was given him, and a new magistrate, favorable to his cause, was appointed. From the regions round about the peasants swarmed in throngs to hear the new revelations. Münzer soon became, as Luther said, both king and emperor of Mühlhausen !

Among the peasants the elements had been in a disturbed condition for some time past, and now a fearful storm was gathering. In South Germany an insurrection broke out, extending east and west, and also northward into the central parts. The demands of the peasants were summed up in twelve articles, many of which were moderate and just in their terms. Thus they demanded that each congregation should possess the right to choose its own pastor. Henceforth they did not wish to be considered as serfs, but treated as free-men, because Christ had redeemed all with His own blood. When Luther heard of these Twelve Articles, he wrote " An Admonition to Peace in Reply to the Twelve Articles of the Peasants in Swabia." He directs his statements at first to the princes and nobles, and says that they, and especially the blind bishops, mad priests and monks, are to blame for this mischief and insurrection, because they do not cease to rave and rage against the holy Gospel ; and that in their secular governments they did nothing but assess and extort, displaying their pride and splendor to such an extent that the common laboring man could endure it no longer. They could not lay the blame of this upon the Gospel, for he had always contended against insurrection and had exhorted to obedience even against tyrannical au-thority. He therefore entreated them to heed his warning, not to despise this revolt, and yet not to fear the peasants ; but rather that they should fear God and for His sake make some concessions, and treat the peasants as one would drunken and erring men, in a kindly spirit, for kindness never suffers any loss.

But the peasants he admonished not to think of their right or power, nor even of the wrongs they had suffered. He warned them against abusing the divine Name, quoted passages from God's Word concerning the rights and powers of the ordained authorities, and showed that the excuse sometimes offered, that the government was a bad one, could in no wise justify conspiracy and rebellion. They might do what God did not forbid, but they should

not bring disgrace upon the Christian name, nor make it
the sinful cloak of their impatient, contentious, and unchristian undertaking. For true Christians did not contend with the sword nor with guns, but with the cross
and affliction. In fact, with the exception of the first
article, their demands had nothing in common with the
Gospel. And if they persisted in their revolt they
would be worse enemies of the Gospel than Pope and
Emperor.

But the peasants persisted in their insurrection.
"Hardly do I look about me," said Luther, "when they
come to blows, steal and rage, and act like raving dogs ;
but especially violent is that arch fiend that rules at
Mühlhausen" (Münzer). The latter had marched out,
on the 26th of April, 1525, with four hundred armed
men, to do battle for the Lord, as he said. Multitudes
flocked to his standard. Cloisters and castles were reduced to ashes. And as yet the princes and nobles were
not sufficiently strong to encounter and subdue them.

Amid these lawless disorders the Elector died in peace,
May 5th, 1525. "Under his firm protection" says Luther,
"the Gospel everywhere happily gained the day. His
name and his great reputation exerted a good influence.
And since he was a wise and prudent prince, no one could
accuse him of harboring heresy or protecting heretics in
his realm. He was a child of peace, and peacefully did
he enter into rest." Luther had charge of the funeral
arrangements. All superstitious ceremonies were excluded. Before his interment Luther delivered two sermons
in the castle church at Wittenberg. To Duke John, the
successor of Frederick the Wise, he wrote : "It looks as
if God had purposely removed him, as he did King
Josiah, that he might no longer behold the wickedness of
the world. During his whole life he governed in a

quiet and peaceful manner, well meriting his name,
Frederick, in word and deed. And such peaceful souls
are not to be begrudged that they no longer live in this
unrest and strife ; for they would occasion us more misery
did we see them passing their last days amid such
turmoil."

But when the revolt and the lawless proceedings of
the peasants grew worse, Luther issued an address
"Against the Plundering and Murderous Hordes of
Peasants." Among other things he said : that the peasants
had merited death in body and soul because of their atro-
cious sins ; that they had sworn to be faithful and true to
their superiors, but that they had broken their vows of
obedience in a wanton and mischievous manner ; that
they instigated insurrections and plundered cloisters and
castles like highway robbers ; and that they endeavored to
cover up such fearful sins with the Gospel, calling themselves Christian brethren, and obliging people to join them
in their outrages. Luther exhorted all Christian authorities
to take up the sword against these mad peasants. They
should be of good courage and use force with a clear conscience. Whoever would fall on the side of law and
order would be a true martyr in the sight of God, because
he would be acting in the pathway of obedience to the
Divine Word. Another reason to justify vigorous action
on the part of the authorities was the circumstance that
the peasants compelled many pious people to join their
infernal league. "To save these poor souls, let every one
who can, strike and slay."

On the 15th of May, 1525, Münzer's army of eight
thousand men was completely defeated in the battle of
Frankenhausen in Thuringia. He himself was captured
and executed. Shortly before this the principal army of
the Swabian peasants was entirely destroyed. Soon the re-

volt was suppressed. The atrocities of which the peasants had been guilty were ofttimes fearfully avenged.

Luther's enemies were soon ready to charge him with the blame of these atrocities. They maintained that his treatise against the peasants was severe and unchristian, alleging that he had preached the shedding of blood without mercy. Even among his friends many were offended. Luther vindicated himself in his " Letter about that severe Book against the Peasants," in which he declared, that if he had advised the slaying of the rebellious peasants without mercy, he certainly did not teach that the prisoners should receive no mercy. Nor would he defend the acts of infuriated tyrants, nor commend their ravings.

And over against the accusations that he himself had incited this conflagration, he could say, "I am of the opinion that no teacher ever wrote so powerfully in favor of the civil authority, for which even my enemies are indebted to me. And who stood up more resolutely against the peasants, with sermons and in writings, than did I?"

CHAPTER XV.

THE step that Luther now took afforded his enemies both material and opportunity for libellous reproaches. In 1524 he had laid aside his monk's cowl and assumed a black ministerial coat. Releasing himself from his monkish vows, he entered into the marriage state on the 13th of June, 1525, at the age of forty-one years.

While he was sojourning on the Wartburg he rejected the very suggestion of such a step. "Good God!" wrote he, "our Wittenberg friends are furnishing their monks with wives; but they shall not force any upon me." And to Melanchthon—to whom he had recommended a wife—he jokingly asked whether he would avenge himself upon Luther by returning the favor; if so, he would be on his guard. Many of his friends and fellow-laborers had already married. And many inquired if Luther did not contemplate taking unto himself a wife. But as late as the 30th of November he wrote : "I am far removed from marrying, for I daily anticipate death and the well-merited punishment of a heretic." And now he took unto himself a wife! He explained his action by saying, "The Lord fairly threw me into the marriage state at a time when I was of a contrary opinion." He speaks of his intention with positiveness, for the first time, in a letter of May 4th, 1525 :

"And if I can accomplish it, to spite the devil, I will marry my Katie before I die, since I hear that the peasants arc continuing their operations. I hope they will not deprive me of my courage and my joy." And to Spalatin he wrote on the 10th of April : "I have urged so many others, for various reasons, to marry, that I shall soon be brought to it myself, especially since my enemies do not refrain from condemning such a step, and our 'wonderfully wise little people' daily make sport over it." The persuasive efforts of his father must have exerted an influence in leading him to this determination, for it seemed to him as if he had regained his son since he had ceased to be a monk.

On the evening of the 13th of June, 1525, Luther invited his friends—among them Bugenhagen, Jonas, and Lucas Kranach*—to his dwelling, to witness his marriage with Catharine von Bora. She was born January 29th, 1449, of an old noble family, and as a mere child she had entered Cloister Nimptsch, near Grimma, in Saxony. In the year 1523 she, together with eight other nuns, had escaped from the cloister and had come to Wittenberg. Here she sojourned in the family of Philip Reichenbach, the town-clerk, afterward burgomaster. Many years subsequent to this act, Luther remarked at table, "If I had wished to marry some thirteen years ago, I would have taken Eva Schönfeld. My Katie did not love me at the time, for I suspected her to be proud and haughty. But it pleased God that I should have mercy upon her. And I was blessed in the step I took, for I have a pious,

---

* Lucas Sunder was born in Kranach, in Bavaria, in 1472, and died in Weimar, Saxony, in 1553. He substituted the name of his birthplace for his family name. As a painter he was distinguished for graceful simplicity, and stood at the head of the Saxon school. He enjoyed the friendship of Luther and the other Reformers at Wittenberg, and frequently introduced them into his pictures.

faithful wife, upon whom a man can depend, and, as
Solomon says, she will do me no evil." The wedding
ceremony took place in the customary manner. Bugenhagen pronounced them man and wife and added God's
blessing. The wedding-rings of Luther and Catharine,
the gift of a friend, have been preserved in the museum
of Brunswick. They are artistically made, and bear the
inscription : "What God hath joined together, let not
man put asunder."

In a fortnight thereafter the usual wedding festivities
were held, to which Luther invited his parents and
friends. From the university Luther received a finely
engraved silver tankard, now in possession of the University of Greifswald. The electoral court furnished a
roast of venison, and the city authorities a generous supply
of wine.

And thus the unprecedented had happened—an expelled monk had married a runaway nun ! Great was
the talk and the commotion that ensued ! Luther's
enemies derisively reminded him of the old legend that
of such a union antichrist would be begotten. Many of
his best friends, Melanchthon among the number, were
troubled about his act. And yet it soon appeared that,
as in other matters, Luther had shown himself to be a
man of firm character, and as one who had done what
was right.

In accordance with the order of the Elector, Luther
remained in the monastery building, which had been
vacated by all the monks. Here Katie established her
household. To-day this stately dwelling still stands,
close to the gate and to the city walls, altered within,
but firm and towering without, a genuine German
home, from which have issued streams of blessing for
the whole world. His married life has become the

model for many thousands. "From that time," says Gustav Freytag, "the husband, the father, the citizen, became likewise the Reformer of the domestic life of his nation, a pattern for filial reverence, marriage, the training of children, as well as for the social family life—the very blessings of his life on earth, of which Protestants and Catholics may alike partake, have sprung from Luther's marriage."

CHAPTER XVI.

THE year 1525 characterized an important epoch in Luther's . life. A controversy with some of his own adherents had been added to his conflict against Rome. Hitherto his activity had been essentially destructive; from this time forth it must needs be constructive. Over against the fanatics and iconoclasts, as well as the rebellious peasants, it was necessary to establish fixed limits, which could not be transcended without endangering the work of the Reformation. The sad experiences of the past few years did not subdue Luther's spirit—for the consciousness that his cause was of God was to him immovable. Yet his tone was not so confident, his spirit and his words not so bold as in the beginning, when he appealed to the German people. Then, the controversies among the adherents of the Reformation, concerning the doctrine of the Lord's Supper, began to separate them into hostile camps, and even to fill their hearts with bitterness.

And yet Luther daily rejoiced to see the Gospel gaining a firmer foothold and developing itself both inwardly and outwardly. The measures of the Elector John, the successor of Frederick the Wise, contributed largely to this result. As chief ruler of the country he showed a willingness to establish a new order of things in the Church, according to the fundamental principles of the Gospel. In these efforts he was powerfully assisted by the Landgrave, Philip of Hesse. By means of such assistance on the part of the ruling princes the cause of the Reformation not only grew stronger in itself, but also as against the Emperor and the imperial princes. But for this new church structure there was demanded less boldness and more persevering patience and a reverent conservatism.

And still in another direction the picture suffered a change. In place of the monk's cowl the habit of the citizen was assumed. Because of this the heart of the German people went out to the great Reformer. As a struggling monk he excited wonder and surprise. But as a husband and father he is loved and revered by the German people. In the times of conflict and development his life was productive of far-reaching experiences and marvellous occurrences. But henceforth a more peaceable career was unfolded, even if numerous conflicts and temptations had still to be endured.

His constructive activity first of all was devoted to the arrangement of the order of Divine Service. Much had already been accomplished in this direction. The congregation took part in the singing of German hymns, but the liturgical services were yet conducted in Latin. Luther established a full order of service in German, and published the new liturgy in a book entitled "The German Mass (Communion) and Order of Service as established at Wittenberg." But he declared explicitly that it was not his intention to oblige all Germany to adopt this order of service. He had in mind another kind of evangelical service, which should be simply composed of the Word and Prayer, and ordered in love. "But as yet," said he, "the people are wanting to carry out such an order of service." He will wait "until the Christians are found who will earnestly accept of the Word and firmly exercise it ;" otherwise a factious sect might grow out of it, if he were to carry out his own notions. For the Germans are an intractable people, with whom it is not easy to begin a new movement unless they are impelled by necessity.

Having finished the work of establishing an order of divine service in German, he next turned his attention to a reform of the parishes. On the anniversary of the 95 Theses, in the year 1525, he submitted the following to the Elector : " Two things yet remain to be done, which demand from your Grace, as the ruling civil authority, order and oversight. The one thing is the miserable condition of the church parishes ; the other, that the Elector should order an investigation of the civil administration of his councillors and other officials, because of the complaints preferred against them in city and country."

The Elector agreed to carry out these wishes, but more than a year elapsed before the matter was thoroughly taken in hand. In November, 1526, Luther again presented the question to the Elector, and maintained that the cities and towns that were able should be obliged to maintain schools and churches, as much so as their bridges, highways, and other necessary arrangements of civil life. The ruling prince should have the sole right to dispose of the monasteries and endowed institutions, and the duty of governing such establishments should devolve upon him, for otherwise no one would care for them. At last, in February, 1527, this matter was earnestly taken in hand, and inspectors appointed. In the month of July the first general inspection was made in Thuringia.

The political situation in Germany contributed no little to the development of the Reformation cause.

The Emperor was hard pushed by France and by Turkey. He could not think of executing the Edict of Worms in all its severity. At the imperial diet of Spire (1526) the resolution was passed that until a general council of the Christian Church be held, or at least until a German national council could meet and decide, each member of the diet should live, govern, and conduct himself in matters pertaining to the said edict, in view of his accountability to God and His Imperial Majesty.

While the cause of the Reformation was thus peaceably making good progress and establishing itself firmly both inwardly and outwardly, Luther was sorely afflicted in body and soul—just after "his dear Katie, by the grace of God, had presented him with a boy, Hans Luther, on the 7th of June, 1526."

In January, 1527, he was attacked by a violent rush of blood to the heart, which well-nigh killed him. But happily, the attack soon passed over. Then he was overcome by anxious forebodings. Great anguish of soul seized upon him, and then followed another rush of blood to the heart.

Concerning the spiritual temptations, Luther says that they were severer and more dangerous than the bodily weakness which overcame him. "And when the spiritual temptation had passed away, early on Saturday morning," thus relates Luther's friend, Bugenhagen,*

* John Bugenhagen, known as Dr. Pommer, or Pomeranus, was born near Stettin in 1485, and died in Wittenberg in 1558. He founded a high school at Belbuck in Pomerania, and started the work of the Reformation. He joined Luther in 1521, being appointed shortly thereafter professor in the university and pastor of the principal church. He became one of the foremost workers of the cause, operating as reformer in Church and school in Germany and Scandinavia.

"the pious Job feared that if the hand of God should again return so strongly he would not be able to endure it, and imagined that the Lord Jesus Christ was about calling him home."

"And so he sent his servant to me early in the morning, bidding me to come to him in haste. Since he said 'in haste' I was surprised, but found the Doctor appearing as usual, standing by the side of his wife, with a quiet and retiring disposition, commending all things to God. For he was accustomed not to bring his complaints before men that could not help him, and whom he also could not help with his complaints. I asked the Doctor why he had sent for me. 'Not because of any evil thing,' answered he.

"After we had ascended to the upper part of the house and had reached a retired spot, he began with great earnestness to acknowledge and confess his sins. The master then desired from his pupil comfort out of the Divine Word—that is, deliverance and absolution from all his sins ; he also asked that I should pray for him, which I likewise desired of him. He requested permission, on the following Sunday, to receive the Holy Sacrament of the Body and Blood of Christ ; he hoped to preach on that day, and did not seem to be concerned about the attack of sickness on the previous afternoon ; he then immediately remarked, 'If God will call me now, His will be done.' I was astonished at this and other statements. After he had confessed and had conversed about the spiritual temptations that had befallen him that morning, with utterable fear and trembling, he continued : 'Many think because at times I manifest a very happy disposition that my pathway is strewn with roses. But God knows what experiences I have had. I have often resolved, for the sake of the world, to manifest a more serious and holy disposition (I hardly know what to call it); but God has not thus endowed me. Thank God, the world cannot truthfully charge me with any vice or immorality, and yet it is offended because of me. Daily and earnestly I implore Him to grant me grace that I may not, because of my sins, give any one just cause of offence.'

"It was now noon, and, at the suggestion of his wife, Luther accompanied Bugenhagen to a dinner at the home of one of the nobility. He ate and drank but little, yet was very agreeable to all at table. After dinner he spent several hours with Dr. Jonas* in his garden, endeavoring to rid himself of his sadness and melancholy. He conversed with the latter upon a variety of subjects, and invited him and his wife to supper. But when Dr. Jonas and his wife arrived at five o'clock, Luther had retired to rest and to refresh himself. He at once arose, but could not remain at table because of the buzzing and ringing in his ears. In company with Dr. Jonas he returned to his room, where a faintness overcame him. He cried out suddenly, 'Oh, Doctor, I am feeling badly; bring me some water, or I shall die.' Frightened and trembling, I hurriedly seized a pail of cold water and dashed some of it into his face and neck as well as I could. In the meanwhile he began to pray: 'Dearest God, if thou hast willed this to be my last hour upon earth, thy

---

* Justus Jonas was born in Nordhausen, Saxony, in 1493, and died in Eisfeld in 1555. He studied law and then theology at Erfurt, and became professor at Wittenberg in 1521. He was present at the Diet in Worms, and also in Augsburg. In 1541 he was appointed pastor at Halle, and accompanied Luther on his last journey to Eisleben. At the time of his death he was pastor and superintendent at Eisfeld in Saxony,

gracious will be done.' And lifting up his eyes to
heaven, with heart-felt fervency he continued praying,
repeating the Lord's Prayer and the sixth Psalm.   His
wife now appeared, and seeing that he was so deadly
faint, she was amazed and called loudly for the servants.
He then lay down and longed for rest, but complained
of great weakness.   We rubbed him, cooled him off,
gave him refreshing drinks, and did what we could
until the physician arrived.   Shortly after that he again
commenced to pray, saying : ' O Lord and dearest
God, thou knowest how willingly I would have shed my
blood for the sake of thy Word ; but perhaps I am not
worthy of it ; thy will be done.   If thou hast so ordered
it, I will gladly die ; but so that thy Holy Name be
praised, whether I live or die.   But if it were possible,
dear God, I would yet wish to live for the sake of thy
chosen people.   Yet if my last hour has come, do as
thou wilt ; thou art Lord over life and death.   Dearest
God, thou hast led me in my work ; thou knowest that
it is thy Word and Truth ; do not permit my enemies
to rejoice, and to boast : where is now your God ?   But
glorify thy Holy Name against the enemies of thy
blessed, healing Word.   Dearest Lord Jesus, thou hast
graciously vouchsafed unto me the knowledge of thy
Holy Name ; thou knowest that I believe in thee, together with the Father and the Holy Ghost, and that I
comfort myself with the truth that thou art our Mediator
and Saviour.   O thou that didst shed thy precious blood
for us sinners, support me at this time and comfort me
with thy Holy Spirit.'   And again he continued :
' Lord, thou knowest that many unto whom thou hast
given it have shed their blood for the Gospel's sake.   I
had hoped likewise to be enabled to shed my blood for
the sake of thy Holy Name, but I am not worthy of it ;

thy will be done. Lord, thou knowest that Satan has persecuted me in many ways, seeking to kill me bodily by tyrants, kings, and princes, and spiritually by his fiery arrows and by fearful satanic temptations. But against all their raving and raging thou hast wonderfully preserved me. Preserve me henceforth, thou faithful God, if it be thy will.'

" He then inquired for the physician. We informed him that he would soon be here. In a short time he arrived, applied hot cloths to Luther's body, administered other remedies, and comforted him with the hope that, please God, there was no danger to be apprehended at this time. In the meanwhile Dr. Pomeranus (Bugenhagen), to whom Luther had confessed in the morning, arrived, and anxiously addressed him : ' Dear Doctor, do you also unite with us in praying that you may yet long be spared, a comfort to us and to many others ? ' To which Luther replied : ' As for myself personally, to die would be gain ; yet to continue in the flesh is necessary for the sake of many. Dear God, thy will be done.' "

Then turning to both friends (Jonas and Bugenhagen) he said, " Since the world delights in lies, many will say that I retracted my teachings before I died. I therefore desire most earnestly that you will be witnesses to my present confession of faith. I say it with a good conscience, that I have taught from out of God's Word, according to God's command, to which work He has constrained me without my will. I have taught right and wholesome doctrine concerning faith and love, the cross and the sacraments, and other articles of Christian truth. Many accuse me of being too violent and severe in writing against papists and factious spirits, and when I castigate their false teachings, impious living, and hypocrisy. I have indeed been too violent at times and have severely attacked my opponents, and yet in such a manner that I never regretted it. But whether I have been violent or temperate, I have never sought to inflict an injury, nor to endanger a human soul, but have rather sought the welfare and salvation of every one. I had purposed to write about Baptism, and also against Zwingli and other fanatics, and I have often complained in tears that so many sects and factions have arisen that corrupt and pervert God's Word, and that would not spare His own flock which He has redeemed with His blood. God has bestowed upon me, unworthy that I am, many beautiful gifts, which he has not given to thousands of others, and which I would indeed like to employ to His honor, and for the use and comfort of God's people, if it be His will. You will not be able to contend against so many fanatics that now everywhere show themselves ; yet I comfort myself with this, that Christ is stronger than very Satan.''

When the feeling of faintness increased he repeated in his prayer comforting words and passages from the Holy Scripture, which he delivered with a fervent heart and with a firm faith and certain confidence in God's grace and mercy. Not long after this he said to his wife : ''My dearest Katie, if God at this time will take me to Himself, I entreat you to be reconciled to His gracious will ; you are my lawful wife—concerning which fact you are to have no doubt. Let the blind, godless world say what it will to the contrary ; govern yourself according to God's Word, and hold fast to the same, then you will have certain and constant comfort against the devil and all his calumniators.'' Soon he again began to pray. '' O my dear Lord Jesus, thou who hast said, ' Ask and ye shall receive, seek and ye shall find, knock and it will be opened unto you,' grant unto me, in virtue of this promise, not gold nor silver, but a strong, firm faith ; let me find, not the desire nor the joy of this world, but comfort and refreshing through His blessed saving Word ; open unto me who am knocking ; nothing do I desire which the world regards as great ; but grant unto me thy Holy Spirit, to enlighten my heart, to comfort and strengthen me in my fear and distress, and to preserve me in the right faith and confidence in thy grace until the end of my life.   Amen."

Hot cloths were again applied to warm his chilled body, and after this had been done Luther asked to see his " dear little son Johnnie" (allerliebstes Hänsichen). The child laughingly regarded its father, who said, "O you dear, poor little child !   I commend you, dearest Katie, and you, poor little orphan, to my beloved and faithful God.   You are poor, but God, who is a ' Father of the fatherless and a Judge of the widows,' will provide for and protect you."   He then conversed with his wife about his silver tankards.   She was much frightened and disturbed at these remarks of her husband, but did not manifest her fears outwardly at being obliged to witness his sufferings.   On the contrary, she comforted herself by saying, " Dear Doctor (Luther), if it be God's will, I would rather see you with Him than with me.   But it is not myself and child alone that are concerned about your life ; many pious Christian people still have need of you.   Do not, then, be worried on my behalf ; I commend you to His divine will, and I hope and trust God will graciously preserve me."

When Luther had partially recovered his strength, on the advice of the physician his friends left him to gain much-needed rest.   On the following day they found him very much better, and in the evening he was able to arise and dine with them.   To Dr. Jonas he then and there remarked, "I must make a note of yesterday, for I received severe instructions, seated, as it were, in a hot sweat-bath. The Lord leadeth into hell and leadeth out again. The Lord killeth and maketh again alive. For He is Lord of life and death. To Him be thanks, honor, and praise forevermore. Amen."

But the end was not yet. That inward feeling of oppression returned, and even increased in violence. He complained to his friends that he was obliged to endure the severest attacks. To Melanchthon he wrote, in the beginning of August, that for more than a week he was tossed about in heaven and hell, and that he still trembled from the effects of his sickness.

While Luther was thus enduring such grievous sufferings, the plague broke out in Wittenberg. At the command of the Elector the university was removed to Jena. Luther, however, remained with his friend Bugenhagen in Wittenberg, though the epidemic reached his very doors. Luther writes concerning those days: "Thus there are conflicts without and fears within. One comfort, nevertheless, we have, over against the ragings of Satan, and that is the word of God, by which we may save the souls of the faithful, even if Satan should destroy their bodies. Pray for us that we valiantly endure the visitation of God, and overcome the devil's might and craft, be it for life or death. Amen." And shortly thereafter he wrote : "I bear God's wrath because I have sinned before Him. The Pope and the Emperor, the princes and the bishops, yea the whole world hate me. And more than that, my own brethren [those differing from him on the Lord's Supper] torment me. My sins, death, Satan with his angels, rage without end. And what indeed could comfort me should Christ also forsake me, on whose account all my enemies hate me? But He (Christ) will never forsake a poor sinner like me."

Before the end of the year (1527) the plague had ceased. Luther's infant son Hans recovered from his sickness, and his wife bore him a daughter which was named Elizabeth.

During these troublous times Luther wrote that grand choral, "the Battle-Hymn of the Reformation,"

"EINE FESTE BURG IST UNSER GOTT. *

1. " A mighty stronghold is our God,
        A sure defense and weapon ;
    He helps us free from every need
        Which hath us now o'ertaken.
    · The old angry foe
        Now means us deadly woe ;
        Deep guile and great might
        Are his dread arms in fight—
    On Earth is not his equal.

2. " In our own strength can naught be done—
        Our loss were soon effected ;
    There fights for us the Proper One,
        By God himself elected.
        Ask you who frees us ?
        It is Christ Jesus—
        The Lord Sabaoth,
        There is no other God ;
    He'll hold the field of battle.

* The English version following is that of Rev. Dr. Joel Swartz. The Rev. Dr. B. Pick has issued a collection of versions, fifty-six in number, in different languages, including Hebrew, Russian, Zulu, etc. It is published by Severinghaus & Co., Chicago, Ill., in pamphlet form.

3. " And were the world with devils filled,
        All waiting to devour us ;
    We'll still succeed, so God hath willed—
        They cannot overpower us :
            The Prince of this World
            To hell shall be hurled ;
            He seeks to alarm,
            But shall do us no harm ;
        The smallest word can fell him.

4. " The Word they must still let remain,
        And for that have no merit ;
    For He is with us on the plain,
        By His good gifts and Spirit :
            Destroy they our life,
            Goods, fame, child, and wife ?
            Let all pass amain,
            They still no conquest gain,
        For ours is still the kingdom."*

In the month of October, 1528, the long-prepared and
extensive work of inspection was begun. Luther himself
took charge of Wittenberg and vicinity, and found the
condition of things somewhat favorable. But other
sections of the country were not in so good a condition.
Thus a contemporary narrates : " Dr. Luther examined
the peasants on the subject of prayer, and also in the
catechism, and that very gently and patiently ; he also
instructed them very kindly in Bible history. On one
occasion he required a Saxon peasant to repeat the
Creed. He began, " I believe in God the Father Almighty," when Luther stopped him and asked, " What
is Almighty ?" The peasant replied, " I do not know."
" You are right, my dear fellow," responded Luther;

---

* The melody to which this hymn is sung was composed by
John Walther, musical director of Torgau, in 1539.

"neither I nor all the learned men can tell what God's power and might is. But do you continue to believe in all simplicity that God is your beloved and faithful Father, who as the Only Wise can and will help your wife and children in every hour of need."

But not only among the common country people, but also among the clergy, did Luther find the densest ignorance. Thus, for example, he found one that could scarcely repeat the Creed and the Lord's Prayer. Some had become notorious by their immoral course of life ; others had to be enjoined from pursuing secular business, such as keeping saloon and the like occupations. In the country districts but few schools were to be found. This crying need led Luther to prepare his two Catechisms in the year 1529. "Help, dear God !" says he, in his preface to the smaller Catechism. "How much misery have I seen, especially in the country villages, because the common layman knows nothing at all about the Christian doctrines ; and many of the clergy are both unapt and unfit to teach. And yet they are all called Christians, have been baptized, and partake of the Lord's Supper, though they know nothing about the Creed, the Lord's Prayer, or the Ten Commandments. They live like cattle and irrational swine, and now that the precious Gospel has come to them they understand how to abuse their liberty in a masterly manner ! O ye bishops, how will ye be able to give an account to Christ, that ye have suffered the common people to be degraded in ignorance, and have not given full proof of your ministry ? Ye permit of but one kind (bread) in the Communion and enforce your human enactments, but ye care nothing whether the people know the Lord's Prayer, the Creed, the Ten Commandments, or anything about God's Word. Woe unto your necks forever !" He then admonishes his fellow-clergymen to have mercy upon the poor people, and to introduce the Catechism among them. And, indeed, next to the Bible, his Catechism, with its pithy, popular language, was most influential in leading to an apprehension and confirmation of the teachings of the Gospel.

CHAPTER XVII.

IN the fall of 1529 Luther accepted an invitation of the Landgrave Philip of Hesse* to Marburg. Here a meeting had been called of all the prominent advocates of the Gospel and the Reformation who were opposed to the domination of Rome. An intimate union of all such into one solid phalanx was an urgent necessity. The friends of the Reformation were divided into two hostile camps. This division gave the enemy frequent advantage for attack. By combating and condemning each other the advocates of the Reformation were inviting the overthrow of their cause.

We have already heard Luther express himself, during his severe illness, concerning the Sacramentarians, *i.e.*, those Protestants who differed from him in their views of the Lord's Supper. At their head, as leader, stood Zwingli,† a native of Switzerland. He had developed

---

* Among all the German princes of Reformation times, Philip of Hesse was the most talented and energetic. Upon many questions and movements he exercised a determining influence, but not always for the good of the cause. His second marriage, though sanctioned by many theologians, occasioned great scandal. He was born in 1504, and died in 1567.

† Ulric Zwingli, the Swiss Reformer, was born at Wildhaus, in the Canton of St. Gall, January 1st, 1484. He studied at Vienna and Basel, and was ordained a priest in 1506, but not until 1516 did he begin to preach the Gospel of the Reformation. In 1518 he was called to the Cathedral of Zürich, which city henceforth

an independent Reformation movement in Zürich, had
gained many friends to the cause, and had proclaimed the
Gospel throughout his native land.   In many important
points he was in accord with Luther, but upon one point
they disagreed, upon the doctrine of the Holy Communion.   Zwingli denied the presence of the body of
Christ in the Lord's Supper.   He maintained that the
words of Christ, "This is my body," etc., denote, "This
signifies my body," etc.   He admitted nothing but a
spiritual reception on the part of the believer.   Luther,
on the other hand, maintained that the salvation wrought
out by Christ's death was presented to the individual
through the distribution of the broken body of Christ
under the sensible mediation of bread, and that faith
was thereby strengthened.   Different explanations concerning the doctrine of the Lord's Supper had given rise
to a violent controversy, and many treatises had been
written on both sides of the question.   Marburg in
Hesse was selected as the place where, it was hoped,
the controversy might possibly be settled.   Zwingli and
his friend Ökolompad* arrived on the 29th of September,
1529.   Luther and Melanchthon, with a few friends,
followed on the next day.   All were royally entertained

became the center of his reformatory activity.   On his return
from Marburg he took an active part in the hostilities between
the Roman Catholic and Protestant cantons, and died as chaplain
on the battle-field of Kappel, October 11th, 1531.

* John Oekolompad, whose real name is said to have been
Hussgen or Heussgen, was born in Swabia 1482, and died in
Basel 1531.   He studied theology at Heidelberg, and under
Erasmus at Basel.   For a while he was chaplain to Franz von
Sickingen at the Castle of Ebernburg.   Called as curate to the
Church of St. Martin's in Basel, in 1525, he remained there until
his death.   He has been termed the Melanchthon of Switzerland.

in the castle and palace of the Landgrave, Philip of Hesse. Luther had reluctantly accepted the invitation, for he anticipated no good result from the interview. Zwingli, on the contrary, had gladly accepted the invitation, and had come filled with joyful expectations that a union could be effected, in spite of a continuance of doctrinal differences. It seemed, therefore, as if everything depended upon Luther.

A friendly and confidential interview having taken place between Luther and Ökolompad on the one hand, and Zwingli and Melanchthon on the other, the great colloquium between these four distinguished theologians was solemnly opened on the 2d of October, 1529, in the presence of the Landgrave, his councillors, and invited guests. In the beginning Luther had written with chalk upon the table these words : " This is my body." He accepted and insisted upon the literal meaning of these words, and said that his opponents should honor God and believe the pure and simple Word of the Lord. Zwingli sought to prove by a number of illustrations from the Bible that the word " *is*" could not have this literal meaning. Thus, when Christ says, " I am the vine, ye are the branches" (John 15 : 5), He does not mean that He and His disciples are actual and real wood of the vine. When he calls Peter a rock (Matthew 16 : 18), he does not mean that the apostle, instead of being a real man of flesh and bones, is a bare stone. But the more Zwingli endeavored to convince Luther of the impossibility of the bodily presence of Christ, the more firmly did Luther adhere to the literal interpretation of the words of institution. And when Zwingli quoted the sixth chapter of St. John's Gospel in his favor, venturing rather boldly to remark, " This passage will break your neck, Doctor !" Luther replied,

"Do not exalt yourself too highly; you are in Hesse and not in Switzerland. Necks are not so readily broken here; spare your proud and defiant words until you return home to your fellow-countrymen. If not, I will administer a blow which will cause you to repent of your remark." Whereupon Zwingli responded: "In Switzerland also justice is administered in equity, and no one's neck is endangered without due process of law. I simply made use of a proverbial saying, which signifies that a person has lost his cause." The Landgrave likewise interposed at this point and entreated Luther not to understand such an expression so seriously.

Zwingli then read a passage from one of Luther's sermons upon John 6, in which he had entertained the same view as Zwingli held, that Christ speaks solely of a spiritual eating, and that the flesh profiteth nothing. To eat the flesh of the Son of God and to drink His blood mean nothing else than to believe that Christ died for us. But now, when Zwingli quoted this passage in his favor, Luther replied: "I care not how Melanchthon and I formerly explained this passage. Prove to me that, when Christ says, This *is* my body, it is *not* His body." And when Zwingli appealed to and quoted the Church Fathers, Luther again replied: "I care not what the Church Fathers teach upon this point; for we have sufficient proof in the Word of the Lord: this is my body." The debate was continued in the afternoon and on the following day, but without leading to the end sought for, viz., union. Luther insisted upon it: "It is written, This is my body; the rest I leave to God."

Finally Zwingli and Ökolompad requested that they might all acknowledge one another as brethren. And Philip the Landgrave also exerted himself to bring about a harmonious agreement. Zwingli declared with tears in his eyes : " There are no other people on earth with whom I would rather agree than with the Wittenbergers." But Luther rejected the proffered hand of union, with the words, " Your spirit is different from our spirit. I am surprised that you are willing to recognize in me, who regard your teaching to be false, a brother. It cannot be that you think very highly of your own doctrine."

Then Bucer,* who had come from Strasburg, advanced and said, " Take your choice ! Either you will acknowledge no one as brother who may deviate from you in a single point—in which case you have no brethren, not even in your own party—or else if you recognize some who differ from you, then you must also acknowledge us." And when at last the Landgrave exhorted them all not to withhold the fraternal love which they owed one another as brethren, Luther remarked, he would not deny his opponents that love which he owed to all his enemies.

But in order that this disputation should not have been held in vain, fifteen propositions, upon which both parties could agree, were drawn up and signed. These are called the " Marburg Articles." The 15th article treats of the Lord's Supper, and reads as follows :

* Martin Bucer was born in Alsace in 1491, and died in Cambridge, England, in 1551. He was educated in a Dominican convent, but afterward espoused the cause of Luther. In 1520 he became pastor at Strasburg, and for twenty years figured as one of the leaders of the Reformation. Invited by Cranmer, he went to England in 1549, and was appointed professor at Cambridge, where he died. During Queen Mary's reign, in 1557, his body was exhumed and burned, together with that of Fagius, who had left Germany at about the same time with Bucer.

"Concerning the Supper of our beloved Lord Jesus
Christ, we all believe and maintain that, in accordance
with its institution, both bread and wine are to be used ;
that the mass is not a work with which grace can be
obtained, either for the living or for the dead ; that the
Sacrament of the Altar is the Sacrament of the real body
and blood of Christ, and that the spiritual reception of
the said body and blood is necessary to every Christian.
And like the Word, so has the use of this Sacrament been
ordained by Almighty God, to move the weak consciences
through the Holy Spirit unto faith and love. And
although we have not at this time been agreed, whether
the real body and blood of Christ are bodily present in
the bread and wine, nevertheless Christian love is to be
mutually exercised, so far as conscience will permit ; and
both parties are diligently to pray to Almighty God that
He will confirm us through His Spirit in the right apprehension of the truth."

A contagious disease having broken out in the city,
the Landgrave dismissed the conference. Luther departed in a depressed state of mind. He said that he
had twisted himself like a worm in the dust, and that
Satan tormented him so that he feared he would never
see his wife and children again. In later years Luther,
reviewing these conflicts, said, "I hold that I have endured more than twenty tempests and factions which the
devil excited—not to mention those of bygone days.
First came the papacy. I think that all the world should
know with how many tempests, bulls, and books Satan
has raged against me ; and when I at times had caught my
breath again, they raged all the more violently, and
sputter without ceasing to this day. Then when my
fears were exhausted, the devil broke in again by means
of Münzer's insurrection, and came near blowing out my

light. But when Christ had stopped up this hole, Satan through Karlstadt broke several of my window-panes, and it blew and stormed as if light, wick, and candle should all be blown away. But God assisted his poor torch that it should not be put out. Then came the Sacramentarians, and forcibly opened window and door to put out the light. They endangered everything, but they did not have their own will and way."

To all outward appearances the Reformers parted in concord at Marburg, and in hope of a fraternal union in the future. But this hope in the realization of an intimate fraternal unity was never fulfilled. Various steps were taken to reach this end. Thus, a conference of Protestants was held in Schwabach (1528), where the articles which Luther drew up, and known as the "Schwabach Articles," were proposed as the basis of a possible league or union. Yet an intimate union between the different leaders and parties was never realized.

CHAPTER XVIII.

WHILE the adherents of the Reformation were thus contending with each other, threatening clouds were again arising on the political horizon. The Emperor called an imperial diet to assemble at Spire * (Speier) on the 21st of February, 1529, in order to adopt decisive measures to suppress heresy. The principal subject named for discussion and action was to make necessary preparation for defence against the Turks. The latter were crowding hard upon the empire and were making steady progress. Hence Luther felt himself called upon to consider the danger. In his pamphlet entitled "About a War against the Turks," he appealed to the nation, with power and energy, to take up the conflict of battle against this fearful and terrible enemy. And in the same year, when the Turks were obliged to withdraw without having accomplished their object, Luther issued another pamphlet called, "Martial Sermon against the Turk." His beloved Germans, said he, would now quietly repose in their accustomed manner, and with a good courage, in all security, would "drink and live high," abusing such great grace, and forgetting it with

* Speier or Speyer is a town in the Bavarian Palatinate, on the left bank of the Rhine, near Mannheim, with a population of about 15,000. In 1689, during an invasion by the French, it was laid in ashes. Little remains of the imperial palace where the diet was held.

ingratitude, saying, " Aha ! the Turk has gone and fled ; what need we care, and involve ourselves in unnecessary éxpense !''

The Imperial Diet, inclined as the majority of its members were to favor the old Church, paid less attention to the common enemy of Christianity and of Germany than it did to the suppression of the Reformation. The decree of the previous diet of Spire, held in 1526, according to which every ruler was pledged to act in conformity with his obligations to God and the Emperor, until a general Church Council could be convened, was annulled. It was now resolved that all who had thus far abided by the Edict of Worms should continue to do so. The other princes and rulers should refrain from further innovations, should not abolish the services of the mass, nor hinder any one from attending the same, and should not harbor or protect the subjects of another ruler where such persons had escaped from his control.

By this act all further progress of the Reformation was hindered ; indeed, the way was open for the return of the Roman Catholic Church to the countries where the reforms had been introduced. The Evangelical princes and rulers could not approve of this resolution, and hence presented a solemn Protest against it, from which act they were first called Protestants. Their Protestation included the following points :

1. That it was not at all necessary to depart from the action taken at the previous diet, in accordance with which the free exercise of religion was granted to every one, until a general council of the Christian Church should convene. No measures should now be adopted contrary to that decree, which was confirmed by oath and seal.

2. The Protestants desire to remain true and faithful subjects of his Imperial Majesty in all things. But the present questions at issue do not concern their worldly affairs or civil matters, but the welfare of their souls and their eternal salvation.

" 3. It has always been found that only a free, general council of the whole Christian Church, independent of the Pope, could definitely decide religious controversies. But no preparation is being made for such a council ; on the contrary, it is now proposed to forbid all those who deviate from the teachings and practices of the Roman Catholics, to develop in their better views—a command which they could not obey because they must then declare their present faith to be erroneous ; such a step would be a denial of Christ and His holy name. If now their opponents, the majority in the diet, should not take these statements into consideration, they, the Protestants, must herewith protest openly before God, their Eternal Creator and Preserver, who alone searcheth the hearts of men and will execute righteous judgment upon all ; and furthermore, they protest before all men and living creatures, that they will not consent to the aforesaid resolution of this Imperial Diet."

Ferdinand, the brother of the Emperor Charles V., declined to receive this protest. In fact, the majority of the diet refused to acknowledge the right of the minority to protest. The Protestants could therefore expect nothing else than the employment of force against them. In order not to be wholly unprepared to meet such a contingency, the Elector of Saxony and the Langrave of Hesse entered into a defensive league with the cities of Nuremberg, Strasburg, and Ulm. Luther, however, would not consent to warlike measures for the cause of the Gospel. He advised all to build upon the help of God, and not

upon the wit or the power of man. Over against the
Emperor, the confessors of the Gospel must keep their
hands free from blood and crime, even if his actions
should prove to be pure threatenings of the Devil. He
exhorted them to cling to God with prayer and in hope,
for they had hitherto often experienced His deliverance.
Luther still continued to repose the fullest confidence in
the Emperor. "The Emperor Charles," writes Luther,
"will be present at Augsburg, and will adjust all things
in a friendly manner."

CHAPTER XIX.

THE Emperor had ordered a diet to convene in the city of Augsburg* on the 8th of April, 1530. The object of the assembly was to deliberate upon the steps to be taken to adjust the differences and reconcile the conflicting parties within the Christian Church in matters of faith and religion. Every one's opinion and best judgment should be heard and received in love and kindness, in order that the real Christian truth might be arrived at.

Before the Elector and his company set out for Augsburg, he requested a meeting of Luther and his friends, at Torgau. † A number of articles should be drawn up, in which the evangelical doctrines should be clearly and firmly expressed, with a view of presenting them to the diet to be convened. They were also to hold themselves in readiness to accompany the Elector on his journey to Augsburg.

On the day appointed Luther submitted to the Elector seventeen articles of Christian doctrine as they had

---

* Augsburg is one of the oldest German cities. It is situated in Bavaria, about thirty miles north-west of Munich, and has a present population of more than 50,000. It has always been, and is yet, a commercial and financial centre.

† Torgau is now a town of Prussia, situated on the Elbe, about twenty-five miles south-east of Wittenburg. Luther's wife, Catharine de Bora, died and is buried here. During the Thirty Years' War the town was almost completely destroyed, and in subsequent wars it suffered severely. Its present population is about 10,000.

already been formulated in the Schwabach Articles. On the 5th of April, 1530, the entire company departed from Torgau and journeyed to Coburg * by way of Weimar, where they arrived on the 15th and awaited the summons of the Emperor. This was soon received, and on the 23d the Elector resumed his journey to Augsburg, accompanied by a numerous retinue of followers.

Luther remained in Castle Coburg, for the ecclesiastical ban and the imperial outlawry still rested upon him. He would hardly have been granted a letter of safe-conduct. But in order that he might not be too far distant from Augsburg, the Elector took him along as far as Coburg. In four days a message could be sent from Augsburg to Coburg.

Luther was well contented with his temporary abiding place. He delighted in the glorious prospect, to be had from the castle, over the productive districts of Thuringia and Franconia, and of the wooded hills which inclose them. The largest building in the castle was vacated for his use; every room was at his disposal, and he was hospitably entertained. "It is a very attractive place," he wrote to his friends, " and well adapted for study. But your absence saddens me. There is a cluster of trees in sight of my window, resembling a small forest, where the daws and the crows are holding an imperial diet. And such coming and going, and such noise and tumult by day and by night, as if they were all intoxicated! Old and young are cawing in such melody and confusion that I have often wondered how throat and lungs could stand

* Coburg is the capital city of the Dukedom of Coburg, situated about 175 miles south-west of Berlin, not far from the Bavarian frontier. It has a population of 12,000. The old castle in which Luther resided for a time is now partly used as a prison and reformatory institution.

it so long.   I have not yet seen their Emperor, but their
nobility and the commoners are constantly in sight. They
are not very elaborately attired, but plainly in a single
color, all alike black, with gray eyes.   They all sing one
and the same song, and yet with a pleasing difference as
between old and young, great and small.   Nor do they regard the palaces and halls of the high and lofty, for their
hall is arched by the beautiful and far-reaching heavens,
and their floor is the meadows inlaid with fine green
branches, and their walls extend as far as the end of the
world.

"They care nothing for horses or armor; they have
feathered wheels that aid them to escape from the range
of guns.   They are great and mighty lords, but what
they have resolved upon I do not as yet know.   This
much, however, I have understood, by means of an interpreter, that they have in view an extensive foraging
expedition against wheat, barley, oats, and other varieties
of grain, and many of their brave knights will execute
valiant deeds.   And I am seated here in the presence of
this imperial diet, to hear and to see, with love and pleasure, how the princes and lords and all other orders of this
empire sing so happily and live so contentedly.   I wish
them good fortune and welfare that they might all be
transfixed on a hedge-fence! I imagine these are the
Sophists and Papists, with their preaching and writing,
whom I must have about me in a throng, in order that
I may hear their lovely voices and sermons, and behold
how useful they are to consume everything upon earth,
and impudently to bid for the whole world."

As soon as Luther had received his books from home
he was again diligently at work.   He took hold in such
good earnest upon the translation of the prophets that
he thought of finishing the work by Whitsuntide.   But

his former sickness again befell him, so that he could no longer work.

It was here that he received the news of the death of his father, who ended this life at Mansfeld, in the faith of the Gospel, on the 29th of May, 1530.

He was deeply moved by this affliction of death, for, as he remarked, all that he was and had, under God, he had received from his dear father. His mother died on the 30th of June, 1531, after he had sent her a comforting letter during her last illness.

Luther, though separated from family and friends, corresponded with his wife and with his friend Weller, who had been received into the family as private tutor of his little son Johnnie ("Hänschen"). It was to the latter that Luther wrote his well-known letter of June 19th :

"*Grace and Peace in Christ.*

"MY DEAR LITTLE SON : I rejoice to hear that thou art learning diligently and praying faithfully. Continue to do this, my son, and when I return home I will bring you some beautiful toys, representing an annual fair. I know of a delightful garden in which many children are found, dressed in golden clothing ; they gather beautiful apples, pears, cherries, and plums ; they also sing and leap, and are happy ; they have beautiful little horses, with golden bridles and silver saddles. Thereupon I asked the man, whose garden it is, to whom these children belonged. He answered, 'These are the children that love to pray and learn, and that are pious.' Then said I, 'My dear sir, I too have a son, named Johnnie Luther ; could not he also come into this garden and eat such beautiful apples and pears, and ride such little horses and play with these children ?' And the man said, 'If he loves to pray and to study, and is pious, he shall likewise go to Heaven, and with him Lippus and Jost [sons of Melanchthon and Jonas]. And when they all return they shall have fifes and flutes and drums, and all sorts of stringed instruments ; they shall also dance, and shoot with small cross-bows.' And he showed me a beautiful plot in the garden set apart for dancing; there I saw hanging real golden fifes and drums, and fine silver cross-bows. But it was quite early, so that the children had not yet eaten their meal. Hence I could not wait to see them dance, and I said to the man, 'I will hurriedly go and write my little son Johnnie all about these things, so that he may pray diligently, study well, and be pious, and also come into this garden. But he has an aunt, Lena, whom he must take along with him.' Then the man replied, 'Let it be so ; go and write him all about it.' Therefore, my dear little son Johnnie, keep on studying and praying, and tell Lippus and Jost that they also study and pray, and then you will all together come into this garden. Herewith I commend thee to Almighty God. Greet Aunt Lena with a kiss from me.

" Thy dear father,
" MARTINUS LUTHER."

"A.D. 1530."

Luther also maintained a lively correspondence with his friends in Augsburg. Here Melanchthon was earnestly at work upon a document which should be both a defence and a confession of faith, and which was to be presented to the Imperial Diet. Following his own inclination and disposition, Melanchthon sought to present the evangelical teachings as agreeing with the universal Christian and traditional teachings of the Church, and the reforms adopted by the Protestants simply as the correction of certain practical abuses. Luther, to whom this document of Melanchthon's was submitted, approved of it in these words : " It pleases me right well, and there is nothing that I would change or improve. Nor would it be expedient for me to do so, for I cannot tread [*i.e.*, write or speak] so gently and so quietly. May Christ our Lord grant that it bring forth much fruit, as we all hope and pray it will."

But at this time it was also necessary to comfort and strengthen Melanchthon, who, because of his anxiety about the proposed confession, the threats of his opponents, and his bodily sufferings, had been troubled with fears and misgivings. Luther wrote to him : "That you should be controlled in your heart by these sorrows is caused, not by the greatness of the work, but by the greatness of our unbelief. For this cause was greater under John Huss, and under many others, than it is with us. But no matter how great the cause may be, He that leads, and from whom the cause originates, is also great ; for the cause is not ours. But why should you torment yourself without ceasing ? Is our cause false ? Then let us retract. But if our cause be true, do we not make *Him* to be a liar, who with so many promises commands us be still and patiently wait ?" And when the Confession was finished, and Luther was requested to give his opinion upon it, he wrote : "By day and by night I am occupied with it ; I consider it from all sides, meditate over it, discuss it by myself, search the Scriptures for proof, and daily the full assurance of our doctrines is growing stronger ; and I am daily growing firmer in my convictions, and will abate nothing, no matter what the result [of the diet] may be." And then he writes again to Melanchthon : "In conflicts that concern my own person I am the weaker, thou the braver ; but in those that concern the welfare of the common cause, it is just the contrary. For thou dost undervalue thy life, but hast fears about the common cause ; whereas I am possessed of a good courage, because I know that our cause is righteous and true ; yea, that it is the cause of God, that must not pale before sin and guilt as I do for my own person. Hence I am here like an observer, free from care, and regard the ravings and threatenings of Papists as nothing. If we fall, then Christ falls with us—Christ, the ruler of the world. And if He should fall, then I would rather fall with Christ than stand with the Emperor."

CHAPTER XX.

On the 25th of June, 1530, the Confession of the Protestants, known as the Augsburg Confession, was read in the German language before the Emperor and members of the Imperial Diet. Dr. Jonas submitted a detailed report of the event to Luther. The latter greatly rejoiced that he had lived to see the day when, in such an assemblage, Christ was proclaimed by His followers in so excellent a Confession of Faith ; and he regretted that he could not have been present to witness this beautiful presentation of their faith. And as little as he anticipated an agreement in matters of faith—for herein they must not yield a hair's-breadth, nor undo what had been done, but rather suffer to the utmost—he nevertheless spoke of a peaceable existence of both Confessions, side by side, within the German Empire. And how deeply he felt concerned about the welfare of his fatherland, we read in his own words when he writes : " We Germans shall not cease to trust the Pope and his Italians, until they bring us not only into a ' sweatbath,' but also into a ' blood-bath.' If German princes should war against each other, that would delight the Pope, that Florentine Scapegrace, so that he would ' laugh in his fist,' and say, ' There, ye German beasts, if ye will not have me as Pope, then take that !' I cannot but care for this poor, miserable, abandoned, despised, betrayed, and purchased Germany ; for I cannot wish it evil, but everything that is good, as indeed I am bound to do for my dear fatherland."

Since there was no hope of an agreement and union in matters of faith, Luther advised his friends to return home. "You have accomplished more," he writes, "than you could have expected ; for you have rendered unto Cæsar the things that are Cæsar's, and unto God the things that are God's. You have rendered obedience to the Emperor by appearing at the diet in face of trouble, difficulties, and expenditure. And unto God ye have rendered the chosen sacrifice which will penetrate to the courts of kings and princes to rule in the midst of its enemies and resound through all lands. Hence, I release you, in the name of the Lord, from further attendance upon this assembly. Return home again ; return home !"

But Luther's friends could not immediately leave Augsburg. They were obliged to await a refutation of their Confession which the Emperor had intrusted to several strict Roman Catholic theologians. On the 3d of August their answer was presented to the diet. The Emperor then demanded that the Protestants should consider the statements of their Confession as having been refuted, and that they should submit to the proper ecclesiastical authorities. Upon this, Landgrave Philip of Hesse secretly departed, although in disobedience of the Emperor's commands. The latter, surprised and disturbed by this act, ordered another attempt to be made to come to an understanding. Melanchthon was inclined to yield in external matters, such as the order of Divine service. But Luther warned him, saying, "I hear that you have undertaken a marvellous work, to unite the Pope and Luther. But the Pope will probably decline, and Luther begs leave to be excused. See you to it that your whole work be not thrown away. If you can succeed in accomplishing this thing against the will of both interested parties, then I will soon follow your example and unite Christ with Belial. . . . Luther is free ; and the Macedonian [Philip of Hesse] is free. Be courageous, and contend manfully."

Negotiations were soon terminated, and the danger which threatened Protestantism from too great concession was now averted. The Evangelical Princes maintained their protest of the year 1529 and the resolutions of the diet of 1516. In closing the diet the Emperor, in his parting address, gave the Protestants a respite for further consideration until the 15th of April, 1531, that they might return to the unity of the faith of the Church, the Pope, and the Empire. This respite was accepted by the Protestants, but objections were entered against the claim that their Confession had been refuted. At the same time Melanchthon wrote and published an Apology to the Augsburg Confession.

Then the Elector John also departed from Augsburg. Very justly had the surname of "the Constant" been given him. On one occasion he declared that "the cross of Christ was worth to him more than his official ermine ; the latter would remain in this world, but the former would accompany him to the stars." To·the Emperor he said, "You will find me in all things to be a true and peaceful prince ; but you will never be able to alienate me from God's Word. For I know most assuredly that the doctrines contained in our Confession will prevail against the portals of hell."

In taking leave of the Emperor, the latter remarked to the Elector, "Uncle, uncle, I did not expect this of you"—a remark which he received silently and in tears. Luther was found in good spirits in Castle Coburg.

On the 5th of October the entire company left Coburg
and proceeded by way of Altenburg to Torgau. Thence
Luther continued and safely reached his family and home
in Wittenberg after a long absence.

CHAPTER XXI. ·

Upon his return to Wittenberg, Luther took the place of Bugenhagen as pastor of the principal city church. The latter had been sent on a mission to introduce and establish the Reformation in Lubeck, as he had already done in Brunswick and Hamburg. Luther finished his translation of the prophets, and also acted as adviser to his ruler, Prince John, upon political and reformatory questions.

Since constant danger threatened the cause of the Reformation from both Emperor and Pope, the Protestants sought to protect themselves by a strong and well-organized league, pledging themselves to mutual defence for a period of six years. To this league belonged Elector John, Landgrave Philip, three dukes of Brunswick-Luneberg, Prince Wolfgang of Anhalt, Dukes Albert and Gebhard of Mansfeld, the North German cities of Magdeburg, Bremen, and Lubeck, and the South German cities of Strasburg, Constance, Lindau, Ulm, Reutlingen, etc. This union was formed at Smalcald (Schmalcalden) near Fulda, in Hesse, Christmas, 1530, and was ratified by all the contracting parties in March, 1531. It is known in history as the Smalcald League.

About this time Luther issued a "Warning to his Beloved Germans," in which he desires to inform them how they are to conduct themselves, if the Emperor, instigated by his devils, the Papists, should begin war against the Evangelical party. In such a case no man should allow himself to be forced into obedience to the Emperor ; for whoever should do this would be disobedient to God and lose his body and soul forever. For the Emperor would then act contrary, not alone to God and divine right, but also to his imperial rights, vows, obligations, seals, and letters. And at the close he says : " This will I say as a warning to my beloved Germans,. that I will incite no one to war or rebellion, but alone to peace. But where our devils, the Papists, will not preserve peace, preferring war, I desire to have it publicly understood, that I have not done this, nor have I given cause to do it, but they have desired it. Their blood be upon their own head. I am not to blame, and have most faithfully done my part.''

Yet the Emperor could not for a moment entertain the thought of waging war against the Protestants, for he was harassed on all sides, particularly by the Turks. His brother Ferdinand, chosen king of Rome on the 5th of January, 1531, advised him most urgently to maintain peace with the Protestants in order that he might be assured of their assistance against the Turks. Thus the time appointed, April 15th, for the submission of the Protestants, quietly passed by. Nor were the enemies of the Reformation encouraged to proceed against them, except it were by their defeat of the Swiss Protestants in the battle of Kappel and the death of Zwingli, on the 11th of October, 1531.

In the spring of 1532 the Sultan made preparations for an extensive campaign against Austria. In view of this a war of German Catholics against German Protestants was out of question. And so it came to pass, after many attempts at negotiation, held in the beginning of the year at Nuremberg and Schweinfurt (in Bavaria), that the

question of union upon matters of religion was postponed
until the expected Council should convene ; and thus
both parties agreed to accept and content themselves with
a political peace and union, which Luther had always desired. This peace was concluded at Nuremberg July
23d, 1532, and afterward ratified by the Emperor.

Luther again had to endure grievous bodily afflictions.
His friends already began to speak of the probable influence which his death would have upon the Papists. But
he said, " I am certain that I shall not die at this time ;
for God will not surely increase the papal abomination
just now, when Zwingli and Oekolompad have died, by
calling me away. Satan indeed would be well pleased, for
he is constantly pursuing me ; yet not his wishes but God's
desires will be fulfilled." At the same time Luther was
much troubled about the Elector. The latter lived to
enjoy the beginning of the religious peace of Nuremberg,
by which a peaceable development of the Reformation
cause was assured for a little while, and the German
people were spared the horrors of a ruinous civil war.
Shortly after that, on the 15th of August, 1532, he was
struck with apoplexy while on a hunt, and died on the
following day. His remains were brought to Wittenberg
and buried alongside those of the Elector Frederick, in
the Castle Church. Luther delivered a funeral sermon
in honor of him who was justly termed the " Constant"
or the " Steadfast." Piety and goodness were the fundamental traits of his character, whereas Frederick was
distinguished by wisdom and understanding. " If both
men," said Luther, " had been one person, it would have
been a marvel. Wisdom died with the Elector Frederick,
but piety with the Elector John."

CHAPTER XXII.

LUTHER lived on terms of happy intimacy with the successor of John the Constant, John Frederick* the Mag-
nanimous. The latter was in hearty sympathy with the
cause of the Reformation, and considered Luther to be
his spiritual father. The wife of the Elector, Sybil, a
princess of the house of Cleve, also took a sincere interest
in the Reform movement and in the fortunes of Luther
and his family. Luther commended them as follows :
" In them, thank God, you will find a pure married life
and course of conduct, a true voice and a benevolent hand ;
they help the poor, build churches and schools, preserve
an earnest, faithful heart, honor the Word of God,
protect the good and punish the bad, and maintain peace
and good government ; their married life is so pure and
praiseworthy that it is a good pattern for princes,
nobles, and every one else ; the princess is a quiet Christian housewife, that resembles, as it is said, a cloister ; at
home they daily read God's Word and have it expound-
ed, they pray to and praise God, to say nothing of what

---

* John Frederick was born at Torgau in Saxony in 1503, and
died in 1554. He became Elector in 1532. Meeting the Imperial
forces at the head of the Smalcald League on the battle-field of
Mühlberg in Saxony, 1547, he was defeated, taken prisoner, and
deprived of his Electorate. He suffered a harsh confinement for
five years, but bravely endured its trials, and was released and restored to his family in 1552.

the Elector himself otherwise reads and writes every day.''

Since 1531 Luther had been diligently occupied with his lectures upon St. Paul's Epistle to the Galatians. With soul-power and earnestness he presented the fundamental doctrine it contains upon Justification by Faith. But the greatest work that he undertook, the translation of the Bible, was nearing completion. In 1534 the entire German Bible appeared in print. It was a stupendous undertaking, and in spite of the many interruptions and the length of time spent upon its preparation, it is permeated by a single spirit, and is a model of German industry and German conscientiousness. Multiplied by the printing-press, God's Word was put into the hands of millions of German Christians. It was now within reach even of the poor man. An immense number of copies were disposed of, not only in Germany but also in adjacent countries. Luther's friend Bugenhagen was so delighted with the completion of the work that he gave an entertainment at his home, and with his children and friends thanked God " for the blessed and precious treasure of the translated Bible."

Shortly before this the Emperor, Charles V., had succeeded in moving the Pope, Clement VII., to take in hand the matter of calling a council of the Church. Luther advised his friends to confine themselves prudently to necessary expressions of opinion, and to await further developments. It was soon manifest that Clement was not in earnest about the council. His successor, Paul III.,* seemed disposed to bring it to pass.

---

* Paul III. was elected Pope in 1534. He called a general council to meet at Mantua, adjourned it to Vicenza and then to Trent, where it convened in December, 1545. He was born in 1468, and died in 1549.

For this purpose he sent his legate, Paul Vergerius, to Germany to confer about the place of holding the Council. In the beginning of November, 1534, he came to Wittenberg, and entered the city in stately array. He was festively received and entertained at the castle. At his request Luther and Bugenhagen were invited to breakfast with him. An account of their interview has been preserved, and reads as follows:

"On Sunday, following All Saints' Day, Dr. Martin Luther was summoned to an interview with the Papal ambassador, who entered Wittenberg on the previous evening with twenty-one horses and one donkey, and was hospitably received and entertained by the commandant of the castle. On Sunday morning early Luther sent for his barber. When he had arrived he asked Luther, 'Doctor, how comes it that you desire to be shaved at so early an hour?'

"Luther replied, 'I am called to meet the ambassador of his Holy Father, the Pope; hence, I must prepare and adorn myself to appear before him as if I were young; then the legate will think, " The deuce! if Luther in his youth has done us so much mischief, what may he not do hereafter?"'

"After the barber had finished his work Luther put on his best clothes and hung a precious jewel about his neck. Thereupon, the barber said, 'Doctor, that will make them angry.'

"Luther responded, 'It is for that very reason I do it. They have more than angered us. Serpents and foxes must be treated in this manner.'

"The barber then concluded, 'Well, Doctor, go with God's peace, and may the Lord help you to convert them.' To which Luther replied:

" 'That I will not do; but it may well happen that I shall read them a lesson and then dismiss them.' "

Luther, accompanied by his friend Bugenhagen, rode to the castle, remarking laughingly on the way, "Behold, here is the German Pope, and his Cardinal Pommeranus; these are God's work and instruments." They then entered the castle and announced their arrival. Forthwith they were received and exchanged salutations with the papal ambassadors, but they did not bestow such splendid titles upon him as was formerly the custom.

Among other topics discussed was that of a council, when Luther said, "You are not in earnest about calling a council; it is only sport on your part. But even if a council should be held, you would simply talk about hoods and tonsure, eating and drinking, and similar fool-work, which we all know beforehand, and which amounts to nothing. But about faith and righteousness, and about other useful and necessary questions, how believers may live in a harmonious faith and spirit—about such questions nothing would be said, for such things do not concern you. We have no need of a council, for we are led by the Holy Spirit unto certainty in all things; but other poor people who are oppressed by your tyranny may need one, for you do not know what you believe. But if it pleases you, by all means call a council; I will attend it, please God, and even if I knew that you would burn me at the stake."

"But in what city would you have the council convene?" asked the Legate.

"Wherever it pleases you, be it in Mantua, or Padua, or Florence," replied Luther.

"Would you go to Bologna?" again asked the Legate.

"To whom does Bologna belong?" inquired Luther.

"To the Pope," was the reply.

"Great God!" exclaimed Luther, "has the Pope also seized Bologna? Yes, I will go there."

Thereupon the Legate remarked that the Pope would not refuse to meet Luther here at Wittenberg; to which the latter responded:

"Very well, let him come; we shall be glad to see him."

"But how would you like to meet him?" continued the Legate; "with or without an army?" To which Luther replied:

"Just as it pleases him; we shall be ready to receive him in either way."

"Do you ordain any priests?" asked the Legate.

"Indeed we do," said Luther, "for the Pope will not ordain any for us.

"And there," pointing to Bugenhagen, "sits a bishop whom we have consecrated."

And many other things were said—the record of which has not been preserved. In short, Dr. Martin Luther told him all that was in his heart, and whatever else was necessary, without fear or hesitation, and with great earnestness. And when the Legate was about to depart, he called out to Luther: "See to it that you be ready to attend the council." To which Luther replied: "I will be there with this neck of mine." Then the ambassador rode away. Ten years after this, this same man, Vergerius, became a Protestant, one of the boldest confessors of the Gospel and an irreconcilable opponent to the papacy.

While the negotiations for a council were being carried on and claimed the popular attention, the cause of Protestantism was steadily progressing. And yet the

greatest hindrance to a more powerful manifestation of
its influence was the division upon the question of the
Lord's Supper. The conference at Marburg led to no
united co-operation of the two parties. And since the
diet of Augsburg, Catholics and Protestants being ar-
rayed against each other in hostile camps, it became
evident that there was urgent need of a union on the
part of all the Evangelical forces. For their dissensions
and the lack of agreement in their doctrines was the very
reproach cast at them by their opponents, and made the
most effective but unfavorable impression upon Catholics.
Luther himself acknowledged this, when he said, " The
gates of hell, the entire papacy, the Turks, the world,
the flesh, and the devil, could not have injured the cause
of the Gospel so much as these dissensions.

Hence Luther now showed a greater inclination than he
did at Marburg to favor these attempts at union. Among
those who were most interested in this work was Martin
Bucer, of Strasburg. To this end he visited Luther at
Coburg in 1530, and afterward declared that he agreed
with Luther that the body of the Lord was really present
in the Lord's Supper, yet so as not to be food for the
stomach. Luther was satisfied with this explanation.
Yet he would not have an immediate union concluded, but
would rather afford more time for mutual conference and
a pacifying of the contending elements. " Thus," said
he, " the suspicion and resentment on our side could
subside and eventually disappear; and then when the
turgid waters on both sides had become clear, a genuine
lasting union could be effected."

Since the return and proclamation of the old Gospel,
nothing gave him more joy and delight than the expectation of realizing a sincere concord after so much
sad dissension. " When this concord shall have been

firmly established, I will sing with tears of joy, ' Lord, now lettest thou thy servant depart in peace.' "

In the fall of 1535 he addressed communications to a number of South German cities, inviting them to send delegates to a conference at Eisenach in the spring of 1536. These invitations were gladly accepted. But Luther, being afflicted with severe illness, could not go to Eisenach. Hence the representatives of Strasburg, Augsburg, Meiningen, Ulm, Esslingen, Reutlingen, Frankfort, etc. continued their journey to Wittenberg, where they arrived in May, 1536. The conference led to good results, and Luther declared, after he had heard all their answers and confessions, that they were now agreed, and that they would be accepted as dear brethren in the Lord. He spoke these words with great fervor and spirit. Capito* and Bucer, the leading representatives from South Germany, began to weep, and then all thankfully united in the Lord's Prayer. Thereupon they partook of the Lord's Supper, and on the 29th of May, 1536, they subscribed to a number of articles drawn up by Melanchthon, and known as the "Wittenberg Concord." The Augsburg Confession and its Apology were received by all as their common confession of faith. By this act unity of belief was established among all German Protestants, with the exception of the Swiss, who adhered to their own confessions of faith.

---

* Wolfgang Fabricius Capito (Köpfel or Köpflin in German) was born in Alsace in 1478. He was for a time professor at Basel and associated with Erasmus. But, called to Strasburg, he embraced the cause of the Reformation, and labored with zeal and energy to advance its interests in that city and throughout Alsace. He died in Strasburg in 1541.

CHAPTER XXIII

SCARCE had this union been effected when the Pope, Paul III., called a general council to meet at Mantua, by which the " Lutheran Pest" was to be stamped out. Upon this the Elector requested Luther to reconsider the evangelical articles of faith, and, in view of an appointed conference at Smalcald, clearly to determine what concessions to make to the papists and what to maintain over against them. Luther himself prepared the so-called "Smalcald Articles," which consist of three parts : 1. About the Chief Articles of the Divine Majesty—articles concerning which there is no controversy ; 2. About Articles that refer to the office and work of Jesus Christ, or to our salvation, from which we can not deviate, no matter what may happen ; 3. About Articles which learned and sensible people may discuss. As the first and most important of all articles, he would maintain the proposition that we are justified by faith in Jesus Christ ; that must not be given up, even if heaven and earth should fall. He declared the mass to be the greatest and most fearful abomination, because it conflicted directly and forcibly against the principal article. It is the foremost of all papal idolatries. Moreover, this dragon's tail has generated a variety of idolatrous vermin. The Pope is not the head of all Christendom by divine right or because of God's Word, for that belongs alone to one, Jesus Christ.

In his reply to Luther, the Elector thanked God that He had given him the power to prepare such pure and Christian articles. He himself was ready to confess them before a council, or before the whole world. But how to act at such a council, this would be the subject of mutual deliberation at a meeting of the members of the league at Smalcald.

In the month of February, 1537, Luther arrived at the designated place. He rejoiced to see so large a meeting of excellent and learned men, such a body, according to the opinions of many, as could not have been assembled at Mantua. A representative of the Emperor was also present.

When Luther had been about a week in Smalcald, enjoying the wholesome surroundings and the bracing atmosphere, he was again overcome by violent pains, which threatened to end in death. On the first Sunday in Lent he had delivered a glorious sermon to a vast assemblage. After that his sickness became so serious that he cried out, "O Lord God, behold I die, an enemy of thine enemies, an accursed and excommunicated one of thine enemy and of Antichrist, the Pope, in order that thine enemy should die under thine anathema, and both of us be judged in that great day!" The Elector hastened to him, and stood at his bedside deeply moved. He sought to comfort him with these words: "Our Beloved Lord and God, for the sake of His Name and Word, will be gracious unto us, and will preserve your life, dear father." Then he turned away, for his eyes were running over. Luther thanked him for his kind visit, and also that he had endured so much for the sake of the Gospel, which precious treasure he desired him to guard hereafter as he had done heretofore.

The Elector replied : " I am afraid, dear Doctor, that

if God should take you away, He will also take away His precious Word."

"Oh no, my gracious Sire," said Luther, "there are yet many learned and faithful men with sincere intentions and good understandings ; and I hope that God will grant His grace that they may become a strong wall of defence for the Gospel. May the Almighty God vouchsafe this !"

In taking leave of Luther the Elector again comforted him, saying, "If it be God's will to take you to Himself, do not be concerned about your wife and children. For your wife shall be my wife, and your children shall be my children."

For one whole week the severest pains afflicted Luther. And as he did not improve he requested that he be removed from Smalcald. The doctors offering no objection to this, he bade his friends farewell, and in departing exclaimed, "When I am dead and gone, remember this : if the Pope should lay aside his crown, if he should descend from the papal throne and renounce his primacy, and if he should confess that he has erred and has plunged the Church into destruction, then receive him into our Church ; but otherwise he shall always be considered by you as the Antichrist."

In company with Bugenhagen and other friends Luther pursued his journey homeward through the woods to Gotha. On the way his condition materially improved, so that he could joyfully write to his wife : "I had been well-nigh dead, and had commended thee and the little ones unto God and my gracious Lord. But God has wrought a miracle upon me ; I am as one new born ; therefore do thou and the children thank God their true Father, without whom they had surely lost their earthly father."

But now, when they had safely reached Gotha, his condition grew so much worse that he bade them all farewell. To his friend Bugenhagen he dictated the following in great haste : " I know, God be praised, that I have done right in attacking the papacy with God's Word ; for it (the papacy) is a blasphemy of God, of Christ, and the Gospel. I am ready to die, if it be God's will."

But he was yet to live. He improved, and slowly continued his journey homeward to Wittenberg. Arriving there in safety, he sent word to his friends that he was gradually convalescing, and that his appetite was slowly returning, although his legs and knees would not yet sustain his body, for he had lost more of his strength than he was aware of.

At Smalcald the allied Protestants resolved that they would not accept the papal invitation to the council. To the Emperor they replied, that the council which the Pope now offered was not at all such an one as had been demanded for so long a time in the German Imperial Diets. They, on the other hand, desired a free council, not in Italy, but on German soil. The Emperor, however, being threatened by new wars, had no intention to compel the Evangelical party to take part in a Church Council. Hence, for the present, it was of none effect.

CHAPTER XXIV.

LUTHER, having fully recovered from his sickness, resumed his former occupation. He was aware that his powers were on the wane, but in spite of this he manifested with his usual energy a great activity in preaching, in lecturing at the university, and in general literary activity. Although old, tired, and exhausted by so many labors, he was always growing young again ; thus he wrote. And when Bugenhagen was called to Denmark in 1537, Luther again supplied his place in Wittenberg. " He preaches," relates a contemporary, " regularly three times a week in the city church. And such excellent sermons does he deliver, that all concede that he has never preached so powerfully before. He points out especially the errors of the papacy, and has a large number of hearers. At the close of his sermons he prays against the Pope, his cardinals and bishops, and for our Emperor, that God will grant him the victory and withdraw him from the influence of the papacy."

Among his literary labors may be noted a thorough revision of his translation of the Bible, a new edition of which appeared in 1541. He spent two years upon this work. In 1538 he published his Smalcald Articles, and in 1539 wrote a treatise " About the Councils and the Churches." In this he developed his idea of the Christian Church as follows : It is the congregation of believers, a holy Christian people which believes in Christ, and possesses the Holy Spirit, who daily sanctifies it through the forgiveness of sins and the laying aside and expulsion of the same.

Nor did he neglect questions of civil and secular interest. Thus, in 1539 he wrote against usury, remarking, however, that his book might touch the consciences of the lesser usurers, but the great oppressors of the people would laugh in their sleeves.

The cause of the Reformation continued to progress, favored by the political situation of affairs, and notwithstanding the controversies and offences within the Evangelical Church. New dangers threatened the Protestants from the Catholic party, but these soon passed away. In Nuremberg a league was formed against the Evangelical party by Roman Catholic princes, with Dukes Ludwig of Bavaria and Henry of Brunswick at the head. The latter strenuously urged a war against the Protestants. It was also rumored that as soon as the imperial armies had defeated the Turks they would turn their attention to the Evangelical princes and their followers. Luther, whose opinion was solicited upon this question, answered that his gracious ruler, the Elector, had a safe and a secure conscience to defend himself, if necessary, against the malice of the adverse princes ; he was also bound to protect his subjects. But it would not be advisable to attack them, for that would be contrary to God's Word, which says : " For all they that take the sword shall perish with the sword " (Matt. 26 : 52). But he no longer opposed resistance to the Emperor, in case of necessity, as he had formerly done ; for the Emperor, said he, in such a war, would no longer be Emperor, but a hireling soldier of the Pope.

But the death of Duke George * of Saxony (in 1539) brought to naught the projects of the Roman Catholic party. Duke Henry of Brunswick, in receiving the news of the death of Duke George, is said to have exclaimed, "I would rather that God in heaven had died." But Luther said, "Duke George presents an illustration in these latter days that is worthy of consideration ; for in a short time a father with two handsome sons has gone to destruction." The oldest of these sons was so embittered that he once sent word to Luther through the renowned painter, Lucas Kranach, saying, "When I shall take the place of my father in power, he shall have a severer enemy in me ; if my father has been like iron to Dr. Luther, I will be like steel." Luther smiled when Kranach delivered to him this message, and said, "Duke Hans had better see to it that he die in a state of salvation ; his threats cause me no fears, for I know full well that Duke Hans will not outlive his father." And so it happened ; for Duke Hans, or John, died in 1537, and his brother Frederick in 1539—both without heirs, and both preceding their father into eternity.

Thus the land and possessions of Duke George were inherited by his brother Henry, who for many years had favored and introduced the Reformation on his own domain ; and thus, after the death of Duke George, the Evangelical doctrines were accepted and the Reform measures carried out in the whole dukedom of Saxony. When some one remarked to Luther that Duke George had died at about the right time, and that thereby the tinder and lunt, which might have caused a great confla-

* Duke George, the Bearded, as he was called in later life, was born in 1471. He was an implacable enemy of Luther and the Reformation, and persecuted his own subjects for their adherence to the new cause.

gration, had been extinguished, he thanked God and said, " The thoughts and projects of the papists are all bent upon this, that they would be willing to destroy the Church if they could only exterminate us Lutheran fellows. But the Lord hath brought their counsels to naught and made their devices of none effect (Psalm 33 : 10).   For He can deprive the mighty of their power and exalt the lowly ; he can also scatter the people that delight in war (Psalm 68 : 30)."

When Duke Henry was solemnly inducted at Leipsic, Luther was invited to be present, and preached in the Court Chapel of the Pleissenburg and in the Church of St. Nicholas.   The entire service was conducted in the German language.   Luther's hymns were sung before and after the sermon, and all the prayers were offered in German.   There was such an immense throng of people that ladders were brought and set up against the outside of the church, that the sermon might be heard through the broken window-panes.   And thus was fulfilled what Luther had prophesied a few years before : " I see that Duke George will not cease to persecute God's Word, His preaching, and the poor Lutherans.   But I will live to see himself and family become extinct, and I will yet preach the Word of God in Leipsic."

In the Electorate of Brandenburg, likewise, was the Reformation cause introduced, in the year 1539, by Joachim II., who had become a convert to the new doctrines.

Under such circumstances, and again harassed by the Turks, the Emperor acknowledged and ratified the Nuremberg compact of a religious peace.   This occurred at the diet of Regensburg in 1541, previous negotiations having taken place at Hagenau, Worms, and Regensburg.   Luther did not anticipate great results from these

negotiations.   The formula adopted at Regensburg
seemed to him to be a vague and a patched-up affair.
The papal doctrines have been deprived of their evil
meaning and adorned to make them more attractive.
"Nevertheless, it will come to pass as Christ says in
Matthew 9, the new cloth upon the old garment makes
the rent worse, and the new wine breaks the old bottles.
Either make it all new or quit patching, as we have
done ; for otherwise the work will be in vain."

At the Imperial Diet of Spire in the year 1544, the
Emperor treated the Protestants very graciously.   In
accordance with a resolution then adopted, Melanchthon's plan of reformation was ordered to be submitted
to a new parliament, to meet at Worms in 1545.   Luther
signed this document.   The Pope violently reproached
the Emperor for his concessions to the heretics, upon
which Luther wrote his treatise, "Against the Papacy
at Rome, Founded by the Devil."   In this he calls the
Pope the most infernal father.   In the strongest expressions he vents his wrath upon the papacy and against the
Antichrist.   And when the Pope summoned a council
to meet at Trent, in the year 1545, Luther derided the
same.   Hearing that the Emperor insisted upon the
appearance of the Protestants at this Council, and that
he was displeased at their refusal to go, Luther said,
"I know not what a curious thing this is.   The Pope
cries out that, as heretics, we are not entitled to seats in
the Council ; and the Emperor desires that we should
attend its sessions and submit to its decrees.   If we consent to such a council now, why did we not submit to
the lords of the councils, the Pope and his bull, twenty-
five years ago ?   First let the Pope acknowledge that
the Council is superior to him, and let him hear the testimony of the Council against him, as his own conscience

testifies against him, then will we discuss the whole question. They are mad and foolish. God be praised !''

The Council of Trent actually began its sessions in December, 1545, but without participation of the Protestants, whose teachings were steadily conquering new territory in Germany. Thus Halle* (the favorite residence of Cardinal Albert and the chief seat of his wanton operations) and the dukedom of Brunswick (after its prince was expelled by the Landgrave Philip and the Elector John Frederick) were won over to the cause of the Reformation. The Archbishop of Cologne and the Bishop of Münster likewise introduced reform measures upon their territory. Hence, in view of all this, the expectation was entertained that the doctrines of the Reformation would yet become the faith of the great majority of the German nation.

* The seat of a university, founded in 1694 by the Elector Frederick, with which the University of Wittenberg was united, by order of King Frederick William III., in the year 1817.

CHAPTER XXV.

THE DEATH OF MARTIN LUTHER.

NOTWITHSTANDING the steady and continued progress of the Reformation cause there was much lacking to complete perfect unity and peace among the Evangelica party. Among many conflicts and trials, Luther had reached his sixty-third year. Frequent attacks of sickness had seriously weakened his bodily frame. Added to this was the anxiety that he felt on account of the course of ecclesiastical affairs, so that at times a weariness of life overcame him. Thus he writes a few months before his death : " I, an aged, used-up, idle tired, and unimpressive man, write to you. And though had hoped that they would grant me, decrepit man that I am, a little rest, I am nevertheless overwhelmed with writing and speaking, acting and performing, as i I had never transacted, written, spoken, or done any thing. But Christ is to me all in all ; He can and will do it. His name be praised in all eternity."

In a sermon he says : " I am tired of the world and the world is tired of me. Hence it will not be hard for us to part, about as a guest leaves his inn." And yet although he was so tired of work and life, he now undertook to arbitrate in a controversy between the Counts of Mansfeld, concerning certain privileges and revenues They finally agreed to call upon Luther to act as arbitrator. He readily accepted the invitation. In company with Jonas and Melanchthon he visited Mansfeld in October, 1545, but as the attempt at reconciliation was fruitless, he repeated his visit at Christmas time. But for the second time it was unsuccessful.

In January, 1546, he went for the third time to Eisleben by way of Halle. In the latter city he sojourned with Dr. Jonas. The river Saale having risen to a flood, he was detained three days among his friends. To his wife he wrote : " Dear Katie : We arrived at eight o'clock this morning in Halle, but could not proceed to Eisleben ; for an Anabaptist met us with waves of water and great blocks of ice, which covered the land and threatened to baptize us. Nor could we retrace our steps on account of the river Mulda, but were obliged to remain at Halle between two streams. Not as if we were anxious to drink of these waters, for we substitute good beer of Torgau and good Rhine wine for the water, and refresh and comfort ourselves therewith, until the Saale shall have exhausted her anger.''

To his friends he said, " Dear friends, we are mighty good fellows ; we eat and we drink with one another, but the time will come when we must die. I am going on a visit to Mansfeld to reconcile the Counts of Mansfeld, whose temper of mind I know. When Christ reconciled the world to God He received His reward in the death which He suffered. God grant that it may be the same with me.''

At the Castle Giebichenstein, near Halle, they crossed the Saale and arrived in the evening at Eisleben. But before he reached that city such a great weakness overcame him that grave fears were entertained as to his life. He had gone some distance on foot, had become overheated, and had then resumed his place in the wagon. " But after that,'' he writes to his dear Katie, " there struck me such a chill blast from the rear of the wagon that it seemed as if my brain would turn to ice. This may have aggravated my dizziness.'' At Eisleben he quickly recovered and preached again three days after his arrival. The business connected with the arbitration proceedings began forthwith, concerning which Luther writes to his wife : '' Here we sit and lie both idle and busy ; idle, because we do not accomplish anything ; busy, because we are enduring untold sufferings, for thus Satan's wickedness torments us. Among so many ways out of the difficulties surrounding us, we at last found one that was promising ; but Satan hindered us again. We then tried another, thinking that we had accomplished it, when Satan once more interfered. We have now entered upon a third, which seems safe and reliable, but we shall see what the end thereof may teach. I beg of you to induce Dr. Brück to persuade the Elector to send for me on some urgent business ; perhaps I may in this way hasten the conclusion of peace. For I am under the impression that they will not permit me to depart without having accomplished the object of this meeting. I will grant them the rest of this week, but then I will threaten them with the Elector's letter. He complains of the jurists as well as of the Jews, to whom the counts conceded too much ; the latter blaspheme Jesus and Mary, call the Christians imps of Satan, drain them of their money, and indeed would kill them if they could.'' He wrote repeatedly to his wife in order to relieve her anxiety concerning him. Soon he could inform her of his anticipated journey home, since the negotiations would be successfully ended. He could not, however, attend the closing session, held February 17th. He was present at the evening meal, but later on he complained of an oppressive feeling in the chest. To his friends he had often said that in Eisleben where he was born he would also die.

And so it happened. Happily had he partaken with his friends of the evening meal. He retired early, as was his custom. At one o'clock in the morning he awoke exclaiming, "O Lord God, Dr. Jonas, I am in pains and fears. I shall now die in Eisleben, where I was born and baptized." Then his friends comforted him, and administered medicines. But again he spoke: "I am passing away; I shall give up my spirit." Then he repeated in Latin, quickly and three times in succession, the words, "Father, into thy hands I commend my spirit: thou hast redeemed me, thou faithful God."

Then he rested quietly and closed his eyes. Jonas and Cœlius asked him, "Beloved Father, will you die faithful to Christ and to the doctrine you have preached?" He answered distinctly, "Yes." Then he turned over on his right side and slept, so that an improvement was looked for. But his countenance was growing paler and his feet colder. He breathed once more deeply and easily, and then peacefully fell asleep. It was between three and four o'clock in the morning of the 18th of February, 1546.

Scarcely had he died when there arrived the Counts of Mansfeld, Prince Wolfgang of Anhalt, and other lords. And from the city many hastened to the house to see their beloved dead.

On the 19th his remains were exposed to view in the church of St. Andrew's, where Dr. Jonas delivered an excellent sermon. At the command of the Elector the mortal remains of Luther were taken to Wittenberg. On the 20th a solemn funeral procession set out from Eisleben to accompany the body to its last resting-place. On the 22d Wittenberg was reached. At the Elster

Gate the remains were met by an immense throng and solemnly escorted through the length of the city to the Castle Church, where they were deposited.   Luther's wife and her sons rode in the procession.

After several funeral hymns had been sung, Bugenhagen, in the presence of several thousand people, delivered an impressive sermon upon 1 Thess. 4 : 13, 14 : " But I would not have you to be ignorant, brethren, concerning them which are asleep, that ye sorrow not, even as others which have no hope.   For if we believe that Jesus died and rose again, even so them also which sleep in Jesus will God bring with him." He said that they had doubtless great cause to be heartily sorry, but that in their affliction they should acknowledge God's goodness and mercy who had awakened this man ; and that he had now secured what he had often sincerely desired.   He then related the incidents connected with the closing days of the great Reformer's life, and in conclusion, against his enemies, quoted Luther's prophecy and memorial inscription : " Living was I thy plague, and dying will I be thy death, oh Pope !"

Then Melanchthon delivered a funeral address, speaking of the office which Luther had held in the Church. " He is to be reckoned," said he, " among the glorious company of elect men whom God has sent to gather and to build up His Church.   Dr. Luther again brought to the light of day the true and pure Christian doctrines which had been obscured in so many points, and he also diligently explained them.   Especially did he teach what real Christian repentance is, and what that certain, real, and constant comfort of the heart and the conscience may be that is troubled because of God's wrath against sin.   Thus, too, did he declare the genuine Pauline doctrine, that man is justified before God through faith alone. Likewise he taught the true adoration of God, and how this is exercised in faith and a good conscience, and led us to the only Mediator, the Son of God, and not to pictures and images of stone and wood, nor yet unto dead men or departed saints.

" And in order that the pure doctrine might be preserved and transmitted unto our posterity he has translated the writings of prophets and apostles into the German language, so clearly and distinctly, that this translation affords more light and understanding to the Christian reader than many other large books and commentaries. And as it was said of those that rebuilt Jerusalem, that with one hand they builded the wall, and with the other they wielded the sword, so did Luther also contend against the 'enemies of the pure doctrine, and yet wrote so many beautiful explanations, full of comforting teachings, and also with Christian deed and counsel, assisted many poor, wandering, and burdened consciences.

" But that some have complained that Luther was too rough and severe in his writings, this I will not discuss, whether to praise or to blame ; but I will rather answer, in the language of Erasmus, ' God gave the world at this time, when grievous plagues and ills had gained the upper hand a sharp and severe doctor.'

" And every one that knew him must acknowledge that he was a very gracious man, amiable in speech, friendly and pleasing, and not at all boisterous, self-willed, and quarrelsome ; and yet withal earnest and brave in his words and gestures. In short, his heart was faithful and without deceit ; his words friendly and agreeable.

" It would take too long to narrate all his virtues ; and yet I will point out a few. I have often found him bathed in hot tears, praying for the whole Church.

And we have seen how great courage and manliness he
has shown, not permitting himself to be frightened at a
little noise, nor discouraged because of threats and
danger, for he trusted a sure foundation, viz., God's
help and support. He possessed also a clear and powerful understanding, by means of which he could soon see
the best course to pursue upon all dark, grievous, and
complicated questions, misunderstandings, and quarrels.

"His books and writings also show how eloquent he
was, and that he may well be compared with excellent
and renowned orators.

"We therefore justly sorrow and lament that so true a
man and endowed with such virtues, who loved us
heartily as a father, is taken out of our midst, away from
life and society ; for we are now like poor, miserable,
abandoned orphans, to have had so excellent a man as
our father, and now to be deprived of him. Hence we
should keep our beloved father in everlasting remembrance, and acknowledge and consider that he was a
precious, useful, and blessed instrument in the hands of
God. We should also with true diligence study and
preserve his teachings, as well as his virtues, which we
need, and which we should take as our pattern, earnestly
and according to our ability imitating the same."

Close to the pulpit from which Luther had preached,
the coffin was lowered into the vault.

The loss of Luther was most deeply felt, with grief
and sorrow, throughout all Germany. Upon Melanchthon his death had made the greatest impression. "The
pain that rages in my soul is indescribable," said he.
"As when two travellers are journeying one and the
same way, and after they have gone a long while
together one of them should fall down dead and the

other lament ; so do I bewail my Luther. And I had always believed that I should be the first to leave this world ; and now I am obliged to survive him ! Who knows what God may yet have in store for us ! For now I see clearly that I have not yet accomplished my work ; therefore the Lord suffers me to live. And I must work while it is called day. I count Luther happy that he did not live to experience a religious war. Perhaps I shall not be so fortunate."

Luther's widow wrote to her sister-in-law : " I readily believe that you feel a hearty sympathy for me and my poor children. For who would not be greatly bereaved and troubled at the loss of so faithful a man as my dear husband has been, who belongs not to a single city or country alone, but who has truly served the whole world. For which reason I am in truth so deeply bereaved, that I cannot reveal my great heart-sorrow to any one ; indeed I know not, and cannot express, my feelings. And had I possessed a kingdom or an empire, I would have given up all rather than to experience such loss and sorrow, as when our dear Lord and God deprived not only me but the entire world of this beloved, precious man. Whenever I think of it, I can neither read nor write, because of sorrow and tears, which God knows, and which you, dear sister, can easily realize."

" The death of great heroes is said to be the precursor of sad events ; what shall we anticipate, after so great a hero has been taken away from us ?" Thus writes a friend of Luther to Wittenberg. A year after this the Emperor Charles V. stood at the grave of Luther, having entered Wittenberg as victor of the battle of Mühlberg (April 24th, 1547), over the forces of the Protestant League of Smalcald. One of his companions endeavored to persuade him to take vengeance upon the dead heretic. To which he replied, "My work with Luther is done ; he has now another Judge whose domain I may not invade. I war with the living, and not with the dead."

OPINIONS UPON LUTHER.

KRAUTH.

" The greatness of some men only makes us feel th
though they did well, others in their place might ha
done just as they did. Luther had that exception
greatness which convinces the world that he alone cou
have done the work. He was not a mere mountain-to
catching a little earlier the beams which, by their ow
course, would soon have found the valleys ; but rathe
by the divine ordination under which he rose like tl
sun itself, without which the light on mountain and vall
would have been but a starlight or moonlight. He w
not a secondary orb, reflecting the light of another orl
as was Melanchthon, and even Calvin ; still less tl
moon of a planet, as Bucer or Brentius ; but the cent
of undulations which filled a system with glory. Ye
though he rose wondrously to a divine ideal, he did n
cease to be a man of men. He won the trophies
power and the garlands of affection. Potentates feare
him, and little children played with him. He h
monuments in marble and bronze, medals in silver an
gold ; but his noblest monument is the best love of tl
best hearts, and the brightest, purest impression of h
image has been left in the souls of regenerated nation
He was the best teacher of freedom and of loyalty. B
has made the righteous throne stronger, and the innoce

cottage happier. He knew how to laugh and how to weep ; therefore millions laughed with him, and millions wept for him. He was tried by deep sorrow and brilliant fortune ; he begged the poor scholar's bread, and from emperor and estates of the realm received an embassy, with a prince at its head, to ask him to untie the knot which defied the power of the soldier and the sagacity of the statesman ; it was he who added to the Litany the words : ' In all time of our tribulation, in all time of our prosperity, help us, good Lord ; ' but whether lured by the subtlest flattery or assailed by the powers of hell, tempted with the mitre or threatened with the stake, he came off more than conqueror in all. He made a world rich forevermore, and, stripping himself in perpetual charities, died in poverty. He knew how to command, for he had learned how to obey. Had he been less courageous, he would have attempted nothing ; had he been less cautious, he would have ruined all ; the torrent was resistless, but the banks were deep. He tore up the mightiest evils by the root, but shielded with his own life the tenderest bud of good ; he combined the aggressiveness of a just radicalism with the moral resistance—which seemed to the fanatic the passive weakness—of a true conservatism. Faith-inspired, he was faith-inspiring. Great in act as he was great in thought, proving himself fire with fire, ' inferior eyes grew great by his example, and put on the dauntless spirit of resolution.' The world knows his faults. He could not hide what he was. His transparent candor gave his enemies the material of their misrepresentation ; but they cannot blame his infirmities without bearing witness to the nobleness which made him careless of appearances, in a world of defamers. For himself he had as little of the virtue of caution as he had, toward others, of the vice

of dissimulation. Living under thousands of jealous a:
hating eyes, in the broadest light of day, the testimo:
of enemies but fixes the result, that his faults were the
of a nature of the most consummate grandeur and fi
ness, faults more precious than the virtues of the con
mon great. Four potentates ruled the mind of Euro
in the Reformation—the Emperor, Erasmus, the Pop
and Luther. The Pope wanes, Erasmus is little, t
Emperor is nothing, but Luther abides as a power for
time. His image casts itself upon the current of age
as the mountain mirrors itself in the river that winds
its foot—the mighty fixing itself immutably upon t
changing.''

BUNSEN.

'' Luther's life is both the epos and the tragedy
his age. It is an epos because its first part present:
hero and a prophet, who conquers apparently insuperal
difficulties and opens a new world to the human min
without any power but that of divine truth and de
conviction, or any authority but that inherent in sinceri
and undaunted, unselfish courage. But Luther's life
also a tragedy ; it is the tragedy of Germany as well
of the hero, her son, who in vain tried to rescue l
country from unholy oppression, and to regenerate h
from within, as a nation, by means of the Gospel ; a:
who died in unshaken faith in Christ and in His kin
dom, although he lived to see his beloved fatherla:
going to destruction, not through but in spite of t
Reformation. Both parts of Luther's life are of t:
highest interest. In the epic part of it we see the in
arduous work of the time—the work for two hundr
years tried in vain by councils, and by prophets, a:
martyrs, with and without emperors, kings, and prin

—undertaken by a poor monk alone, who carried it out
under the ban both of the Pope and the empire. In the
second we see him surrounded by friends and disciples,
always the spiritual head of his nation, and the revered
adviser of princes and preacher of the people ; living in
the same poverty as before, and leaving his descendants
as unprovided for as Aristides left his daughter. So
lived and died the greatest hero of Christendom since
the apostles ; the restorer of that form of Christianity
which now sustains Europe, and (with all its defects)
regenerating and purifying the whole human race ; the
founder of the modern German language and literature ;
the first speaker and debater of his country ; and, at the
same time, the first writer in prose and verse of his age.''

HARE.

" As he has said of St. Paul's words, his own are not
dead words, but living creatures, and have hands and
feet. It no longer surprises us that this man who wrote
and spoke thus, although no more than a poor monk,
should have been mightier than the Pope, and the
Emperor to boot, with all their hosts, ecclesiastical and
civil—that the rivers of living water should have swept
half Germany, and in the course of time the chief part
of Northern Europe, out of the kingdom of darkness
into the region of Evangelical light. No day in spring,
when life seems bursting from every bud and gushing
from every pore, is fuller of life than his pages ; and if
they are not without the strong breezes of spring, these
too have to bear their part in the work of purification.
How far superior his expositions of Scriptures are in the
deep and living apprehension of the primary truths of
the Gospel to those of the best among the Fathers, even
of Augustine. If we would do justice to any of the

'master minds in history, we must compare them wit
their predecessors.   When we come upon these truths i
Luther, after wandering through the dusky twilight (
the preceding centuries, it seems almost like the sui
burst of a new revelation or rather as if the sun, whic
set when St. Paul was taken away from the earth, ha
suddenly started up again.   Verily, too, it does us goo(
when we have been walking about among those wl
have only dim guesses as to where they are, or whith(
they are going, and who halt and look back, and tui
aside at every other step, to see a man taking his stan
on the Eternal Rock, and gazing steadfastly with ui
sealed eyes on the very Sun of righteousness."

HEINE.

" He created the German language.   He was not on:
the greatest but the most German man of our histor:
In his character all the faults and all the virtues of tl
Germans are combined on the largest scale.   Then 1
had qualities which are very seldom found united, whic
we are accustomed to regard as irreconcilable antag(
nisms.   He was, at the same time, a dreamy mystic an
a practical man of action.   His thoughts had not onl
wings, but hands.   He spoke and he acted.   He was n(
only the tongue, but the sword of his time.   When l
had plagued himself all day long with his doctrinal di
tinctions, in the evening he took his flute and gazed :
the stars, dissolved in melody and devotion.   He coul
be as soft as a tender maiden.   Sometimes he was wil
as the storm that uproots the oak, and then again he w:
gentle as the zephyr that dallies with the violet.   H
was full of the most awful reverence and of self-sacrifi(
in honor of the Holy Spirit.   He could merge himse
entire, in pure spirituality.   And yet he was well a(

quainted with the glories of this world, and knew how
to prize them.   He was a complete man, I would say an
absolute man, one in whom matter and spirit were not
divided.   To call him a spiritualist, therefore, would
be as great an error as to call him a sensualist.   How
shall I express it ?   He had something original, incom-
prehensible, miraculous, such as we find in all providential men—something invincible, spirit-possessed.''

HALLAM.

''A better tone began with Luther.   His language
was sometimes rude and low, but persuasive, artless,
powerful.   He gave many useful precepts, as well as
examples, for pulpit eloquence.   In the history of the
Reformation, Luther is incomparably the greatest name.
We see him, the chief figure of a group of gownsmen,
standing in contrast on the canvas with the crowned
rivals of France and Austria, and their attendant war-
riors, but blended in the unity of that historic picture.
It is admitted on all sides that he wrote his own language
with force, and he is reckoned one of its best models.
The hymns in use with the Lutheran Church, many of
which are his own, possess a simple dignity and devout-
ness, never before excelled in that class of poetry, and
alike distinguished from the poverty of Sternhold or
Brady.   It is not to be imagined that a man of his
vivid parts fails to perceive an advantage, in that close
grappling, sentence by sentence, with an adversary,
which fills most of his controversial writings, and in
scornful irony he had no superior.''

CARLYLE.

''There was born here, once more, a mighty man ;
whose light was to flame as the beacon over long cen-

turies and epochs of the world ; the whole world and i
history was waiting for this man. It is strange, it
great. It leads us back to another birth-hour, in a sti
meaner environment, eighteen hundred years ago, ι
which it is fit that we *say* nothing, that we think only i
silence ; for what words are there ! The Age of Miri
cles past ? The Age of Miracles is forever here !

"I will call this Luther a true great man, great i
intellect, in courage, affection, and integrity, one of oι
most lovable and precious men. Great not as a hew
obelisk, but as an Alpine mountain, so simple, honesi
spontaneous, not setting up to be great at all ; there fc
quite another purpose than being great ! Ah, yeι
unsubduable granite, piercing far and wide into th
heavens ; yet in the clefts of it fountains, green beaut
ful valleys with flowers ! A right spiritual Hero an
Prophet ; once more a true son of Nature and Fact, fc
whom these centuries and many that are to come yι
will be thankful to heaven."

BOSSUET.

"In the time of Luther, the most violent rupture an
greatest apostasy occurred which had perhaps ever bee
seen in Christendom. The two parties who have calle
themselves reformed have alike recognized him as th
author of this new Reformation. It is not alone h
followers, the Lutherans who have lavished upon hii
the highest praises. Calvin frequently admires his vii
tues, his magnanimity, his constancy, the incomparabl
industry which he displayed against the Pope. He i
the trumpet, or rather he is the thunder—he is th
lightning which has roused the world from its lethargy
it was not so much Luther that spoke, as God whos
lightnings burst from his lips. And it is true that h

had a strength of genius, a vehemence in his discourses, a living and impetuous eloquence which entranced and ravished the people."

CALVIN.

"We sincerely testify that we regard him as a noble apostle of Christ, by whose labor and ministry the purity of the Gospel has been restored in our times. If any one will carefully consider what was the state of things at the period when Luther arose, he will see that he had to contend with almost all the difficulties which were encountered by the apostles. In one respect, indeed, his condition was worse and harder than theirs. There was no kingdom, no principality against which they had to declare war. Whereas Luther could not go forth, except by the ruin and destruction of that empire which was not only the most powerful of all, but regarded all the rest as obnoxious to itself."

BANCROFT.

"Luther was more dogmatical than his opponents; though the deep philosophy with which his mind was imbued repelled the use of violence to effect conversion in religion. He was wont to protest against propagating reform by persecution and massacres; and with wise moderation, an admirable knowledge of human nature, a familiar and almost ludicrous quaintness of expression, he would deduce from his great principle of justification by faith alone, the sublime doctrine of freedom of conscience."

D'AUBIGNÉ.

. "Luther proved through divine grace the living influence of Christianity, as no preceding doctor, perhaps,

had ever felt it before. The Reformation sprang livin;
from his own heart, where God Himself had placed it
' Some advised the Evangelical princes to meet Charle
sword in hand. But this was mere worldly counsel, an
the great Reformer Luther, whom so many are please
to represent as a man of violent temper, succeeded i:
silencing these rash counsellors.' If in the history o
the world there be an individual we love more tha;
another, it is he. Calvin we venerate more, but Luthe
we love more."

GELZER.

" If we recall among other great names in Germa;
history the Reformers Melanchthon and Zwingli, th
Saxon Electors, Frederick the Wise and John the Con
stant, Gustavus Adolphus and Frederick the Great, o
among intellectual celebrities, Klopstock and Lessing
Haman and Herder, Goethe and Schiller, or turn to th
great religious reformers of the last centuries, Spener
Franke, Zinzendorf, Bengel, and Lavater, they all ex
hibit many features of relationship with Luther, and i:
some qualities may even surpass him, but not one stand
out a *Luther*."

HERDER.

" Luther has long been recognized as teacher of th
German nation, nay, as co-reformer of all of Europe tha
is this day enlightened. He was a great man and a grea
patriot. Even nations that do not embrace the principle
of his religion, enjoy the fruits of his Reformation. A
a preacher, Luther spoke the simple, strong, unadorne
language of the understanding ; he spoke from the heart
not from the head and from memory. His sermons hav
long been the models especially of those preachers in ou
Church who are of stable minds."

RANKE.

" Throughout we see Luther directing his weapons on both sides—against the Papacy, which sought to re-conquer the world then struggling for its emancipation—and against the sects of many names which sprang up beside him, assailing Church and State together. The great Reformer, if we may use an expression of our days, was one of the greatest conservatives that ever lived."

MELANCHTHON.

" Luther is too great, too wonderful for me to depict in words. If there be a man on earth I love with my whole heart, that man is Luther. One is an interpreter, one a logician, another an orator, affluent and beautiful in speech, but Luther is all in all—whatever he writes, whatever he utters, pierces to the soul, fixes itself like arrows in the heart—he is a miracle among men."

ERASMUS.

" All the world is agreed among us in commending his moral character. He hath given us good advice on certain points ; and God grant that his success may be equal to the liberty which he hath taken. Luther hath committed two unpardonable crimes : he hath touched the Pope upon the crown, and the monks upon the belly."

COLERIDGE.

" How would Christendom have fared without a Luther ? What would Rome have done and dared but for the ocean of the Reformed that ROUNDS her. Luther lives yet—not so beneficially in the Lutheran Church as

out of it—an antagonistic spirit to Rome, and a purif
ing and preserving spirit in Christendom at large.''

FROUDE.

" Had there been no Luther, the English, America
and German peoples would be thinking differentl
would be acting differently, would be altogether differe
men and women from what they are at this moment."

LESSING.

" In such reverence do I hold Luther that I rejoice
having been able to find some defects in him ; for
have, in fact, been in imminent danger of making hi
an object of idolatrous veneration.''

STOLBERG.

" Against Luther's person I would not cast a ston
In him I honor, not alone one of the grandest spiri
that ever lived, but a great religiousness also, whi
never forsook him.''

KAHNIS.

" Nothing but the narrowness of party can deny th
there are respects in which no other reformer can be
comparison with Luther, as *the* person of the Reform
tion."

WIELAND.

" So great was Luther, in whatever aspect we vie
him, so worthy of admiration, so deserving of univers
gratitude, alike great as a man, a citizen, and a scholar.

CHRONOLOGICAL TABLE OF EVENTS THE LIFE OF MARTIN LUTHER.

1483. November 10th. Martin Luther is born at Eisleben, an

1483.   "   11th. Baptized in the Church of St. Peter and
Paul.

1497. Attends the instruction of the " Null-brothers" at Magdebu

1498. Is sent to school at Eisenach—Ursula Cotta.

1501. Attends the University at Erfurt.

1502. Obtains his first degree : Bachelor of Philosophy.

1504. Secures his second degree : Master of Arts or Philosophy.

1505. July 16th. Enters the Augustinian Cloister at Erfurt.

1506. Ends his novitiate and becomes a monk.

1507. May 2d. Is ordained a priest.

1508. Appointed Professor of Philosophy in Wittenberg Univers

1509. March 9th. Receives his degree as Bachelor of Theology.

1511. Visits Rome on business for the Augustinians.

1512. October 18th. Receives his degree as Doctor of Sacred '
ology.

1516. Publishes " German Theology."

1517. Translates and publishes the Penitential Psalms.

1517. October 31st. Attaches his 95 Theses to the doors of the C
Church.

1518. August 7th. Summoned to appear in Rome.

1518. October. Meets Cajetan in Augsburg.

1519. January. Confers with Miltitz at Altenburg.

1519. July 4th-16th. Disputes with Eck at Leipsic.

1520. August. Publishes : " To the Christian Nobles of the Ger
Nation ;" " The Babylonian Captivity of the Church ;" "
Liberty of the Christian."

1520. November 10th. Luther burns the Papal Bull.

1521. April 17th and 18th. Appears at the Diet of Worms.

1521. May 5th. Luther on the Wartburg.

1521. May 8th. Charles V. issues his edict against Luther.

1521. May. Begins the Translation of the Scriptures.

1522. September 21st. The New Testament published.

1522. Luther visits Wittenberg and preaches against the iconoclasts.

1522. March. Returns to Wittenberg and restores order.

1524. Publishes a German hymn-book.

1524. Proceeds against the fanatical " New Prophets."

1524. October 9th. Lays aside his monk's cowl.

1525. June 13th. Marries Catharine de Bora and establishes a home.

1526. June 7th. Hans Luther is born.

1527. January. Suffers from serious illness.

1528. October. Inspects the churches of Wittenberg and vicinity.

1529. Prepares and publishes his two Catechisms.

1529. October. Attends the conference at Marburg.

1530. April–October Luther in Coburg. (Diet at Augsburg.)

1534. Publishes the entire Bible in German.

1536. May. Confers with South German theologians. Wittenberg Concord.

1537. February. Luther in Smalcald. Smalcald Articles.

1545. October. Called to arbitrate between the Counts of Mansfeld.

1545. Christmas. Goes again to Mansfeld.

1546. January. Repeats his visit to Mansfeld.

1546. January 17th. Preaches for the last time in Wittenberg.

1546. January 28th. Arrives in Eisleben.

1546. February 16th. Establishes peace between the Counts of Mansfeld.

1546. February 18th. Dies in Eisleben.

1546. February 22d. Martin Luther is buried in the Castle Church at Wittenberg.

INDEX.

A.

ADRIAN VI., Pope, 119; threatens Luther, 120.
ALBERT, Archbishop of Mayence, 11; sells indulgences at Halle, 97.
ALBERT, of Brandenburg, 121.
ALL-SAINTS' Day, observed, 7.
ALTENBURG, 60.
AMSDORF, 102.
ANTICHRIST, 73; against his bulls, 79.
APOLOGY to the Augsburg Confession, 170; adopted at Wittenberg, 181.
ARISTOTLE, rejected by Luther, 41.
AUGSBURG, 52; the present city of, 162.
AUGSBURG, Confession of, drawn up by Melanchthon, 166; approved by Luther, 166; presented to the Diet, 168; adopted at Wittenberg, 181.
AUGSBURG, The Diet of, 162.
AUGUSTINIAN monks, 27; their reputation, 29; origin, 29; dispute within the order, 37.

B.

"BABYLONIAN Captivity of the Church," 75.
BANCROFT, 208.
"BATTLE-HYMN of the Reformation," 147; its versions, 147; its melody, 148.
"BEAR, The Black," inn at Jena, 108.
BERKA, 91.
BERLEPSCH, Hans von, 93.
BIBLE, The, discovered by Luther, 28; translated by, 97; the whole in print, 176; revised, 186.
BISHOPS converted to Protestantism, 121.
BORNA, 105.
BOSSUET, 207.
BRANDENBURG, The Bishop of, 69.
BRUNSWICK, Reformation adopted in, 191.
BUCER, Martin, at Marburg, 155; visits Luther at Coburg, 180.
BUGENHAGEN, 133; at Luther's marriage, 134; note upon, 139; sent to Lubeck, 172; called to Denmark, 186; preaches Luther's funeral sermon, 196.
BULL of Excommunication, 76; how received, 77; how executed, 79.
BUNSEN, 208.

C.

CAJETAN, 50; meets [...]
ens him, 54; prefer[...]
CALVIN, 208.
CAPITO, Wolfgang, 18[...]
CARLYLE, 206.
CASTLE Church at Wi[...]
CATECHISMS of Luthe[...]
derful influence, 15[...]
CHARITY students, 23[...]
CHARLES V., 61; sum[...]
keeps his word, 85[...]
opinion of Luther[...]
sentence, 90; issu[...]
grants a respite, 170[...]
CHURCH, The, in need [...]
the Pope alone, 73.
CITIES espousing the R[...]
121.
"CHRISTIAN nobles o[...]
tion, To the," 71.
"CHRISTIAN, The, a [...]
CLEMENT VII., Pope, [...]
CONFESSION of sin, 97[...]
COBURG, City and Ca[...]
COLERIDGE, 210.
COTTA, Ursula, 23; p[...]

D.

D'AUBIGNÉ, 208.
DE BORA, Catharine, [...]
Luther's sickness, [...]
Torgau, 162; effect[...]
upon, 199.
DOMINICANS, The, 69[...]
DÜRER, Albert, 93.

E.

EBERNBURG, 70.
ECK, Dr., 62; disput[...]
63; with Luther, 6[...]
69; returns with th[...]
EDICT of Spire (1526)[...]
EDICT of Worms, 94.
"EINE FESTE BURG," [...]
147; its melody, 14[...]
EISENACH, 22; its ch[...]
Luther's sickness [...]
preaching at, 91.

EISLEBEN, 18; visited by a conflagration, 19.
ERASMUS, 122; opinion upon Luther, 210.
ERFURT, University of, 25.
ERICH, Duke of Brunswick, 89.
EXCOMMUNICATION, 67.

F.

FABLE about the crows, 163.
FAITH, the central point, 40; a remarkable memorial of, 105.
FALSE Prophets, 103; their views, 125.
FANATICISM, Religious, 103; illustrated, 124.
FERDINAND at Worms, 86; at Spire, 160.
FORGIVENESS of sins, 40; alone by God, 14.
FORCE, The use of, protested against by Luther, 160; reiterated, 187.
FREDERICK the Wise, 36; receives Luther's theses, 47; refuses Cajetan's demands, 56; Imperial Vicar, 61; conceives the seizure of Luther, 95; restrains Luther, 98; forbids his return, 104; his death, 129.
FREYTAG, Gustav, on Luther's home, 135.
FROUDE, 211.
FRUNDSBERG, George von, 85.

G.

GALATIANS, Lectures upon, 176.
GELZER, 209.
GEORGE, Duke, 65; prefers charges, 69; commented upon by Luther, 106; his treatment of Luther, 188; his death, 188.
"GERMAN Mass, The," 137.
GERMANS despised in Rome, 39; "an intractable people," 138.
GOOD works, 9.

H.

HALLAM, 206.
HALLE, indulgences sold at, 97; Reformation introduced, 191; its university united with Wittenberg, 191; visited by Luther, 193.
HARE, 204.
HEINE, 205.
HENRY VIII. of England, 118.
HENRY, Elector of Saxony, 188; inducted, 189; assists the Reformation, 188.
HERDER, 209.
HEROSTRATUS, 52.
HERSFELD, 91.
HUNTING, Sport of, 95.
HUSS, John, 65; note upon, 68.
HUTTEN, Ulrich von, 69; against the Romans, 71; note upon, 71; advises the use of force, 80.
HYMNS, Influence of, 33; first collection of German, 122; used at Leipsic, 189.

I.

ICONOCLASM, 102.
IGNORANCE, Religious, illustrated, 149.
INDULGENCES, 8; warned against by Luther, 8; their origin, 9; a matter of profit, 10; sold at tariff rates, 13; denounced by Luther, 14; sold at Halle, 97.
INKSTAND story, 97.
INSPECTION, General, of the churches ordered, 138.

J.

JENA, 108.
JOHN the Constant, 118; helpful to the Reformation, 126; his character, 170; parts with Charles V., 170; his private and family life, 175; comforts Luther, 184.
JÜTERBOCK, 9.
JONAS, Justus, 141; preaches Luther's funeral sermon, 195.
JULIUS, II., Pope, 38; begins St. Peter's Church, 39; lays its corner-stone, 10.
JUSTIFICATION by Faith, 38; becomes fixed in Luther's soul, 40; the doctrine fully developed, 176.

K.

KAHNIS, 211.
KARLSTADT, Dr., 62; disputes with Eck, 63; begins radical reforms, 102; again creates disturbances, 124; note upon, 124; stormy interview with Luther, 126; leaves the country, 127.
KESSLER, John Jacob, 109.
KRANACH, Lucas, 133.
KRAUTH, 201.

L.

LANDSTUHL, 70.
LEAGUE, A Defensive, formed at Spire, 160.
LEIPSIC, 63.
LEO X., Pope, completes St. Peter's Church, 10; his record, 10; partner with Albert of Mayence, 11; his opinion of Luther, 48; cites Luther to appear, 48; instructs the Elector, 49; requests an Imperial tax, 49; proceeds against Luther, 76; issues another bull, 81.
LESSING, 211.
"LIBERTY of the Christian, The," 77.
LINK, 51; at Augsburg, 55.
LORD's Supper, The, 67; Zwingli's view of, 152; Luther's view of, 153; in the Marburg Articles, 156; differences among Protestants upon, 180.
LUTHER, Hans, at Möhra, 18; false reports concerning 18; removes to Eisleben, 18; to Mansfeld, 19; struggle for existence; 20; is prosperous, 25; designs with Martin, 26; refuses his

consent, 30 ; loses two sons, 30 ; present at Martin's ordination, 32 ; desires his marriage, 133 ; dies, 165.

LUTHER, Heinz, 18 ; visited by Martin Luther, 91.

LUTHER, Jacob, 19.

LUTHER, /Martin, his birth and parentage, 17 ; his ancestors, 18 ; is baptized, 19 ; at Mansfeld, 19 ; his home training, 20 ; school training, 21 ; at Magdeburg, 22 ; at Eisenach, 22 ; a charity scholar, 22 ; is befriended by Ursula Cotta, 23 ; receives further aid, 24 ; goes to Erfurt University, 25 ; his favorite studies, 25 ; obtains his degrees, 26 ; studies law, 26 ; enters a monastery, 27 ; reasons for the step, 27-29 ; discovers a Latin Bible, 28 ; his providential experiences, 29 ; in the cloister, 30 ; menial labors, 31 ; becomes a monk and ordained a priest, 31 ; his soul conflicts, 32 ; receives light, 33 ; appointed professor at Wittenberg, 36 ; impressions of the city, 36 ; obtains his first theological degree, 37 ; returns to Erfurt, 37 ; visits Rome, 37 ; soul experiences, 38 ; studies Hebrew, 39 ; returns to Wittenberg, 39 ; obtains his second theological degree, 39 ; lectures upon the Psalms, 40 ; explains law and gospel, 40 ; reads Tauler, 41 ; publishes his "German Theology," 41 ; publishes his 95 Theses, 7 ; preaches against indulgences, 8 ; attacks Tetzel's traffic, 14 ; influenced by Tauler, 42 ; stands alone at first, 43 ; sends theses to Pope and bishops, 44 ; still respects the Pope, 46 ; replies to Tetzel's counter-theses, 47 ; preaches at Weimar, 51 ; meets Cajetan, 53 ; leaves Augsburg on horseback, 56 ; appeals to a council, 57 ; confers with Miltitz, 60 ; disputes with Eck, 64 ; his personal appearance, 64 ; accused of being a Hussite, 68 ; appeals to the Christian nobility, 71 ; receives the papal bull, 77 ; writes to the Pope, 77 ; burns the Pope's bull, 79 ; releases himself from monastic vows, 80 ; opposes the use of force, 80 ; at Worms, 80-82, sick at Eisenach, 84 ; confronts the diet, 86 ; journey home, 91 ; visits Möhra, 91 ; is carried to the Wartburg, 92 ; his treatment there, 95 ; tormented by the devil, 96 ; begins translating the Bible, 97 ; writes against Albert of Mayence, 97 ; publishes the New Testament, 101 ; visits Wittenberg suddenly, 102 ; leaves the Wartburg, 104 ; addresses the Elector, 105 ; incident at Jena, 109 ; his hospitality, 114 ; meets the false prophets, 117 ; contends with Henry VIII., 118 ; reforms the Church service, etc., 122 ; proceeds against the fanatics, 125 ; admonishes the nobles and peasants, 128 ; lays aside his monk's cowl and marries Catharine de Bora, 132 ; estab-

lishes a home, in German, and clerical a son, 139 ; ser his faith, 143 Burg," 147 ; 148 ; goes to mented with the Schwabac against the Tu using force, 16 translates the parents, 165 ; v 165 ; strength returns to Wi place of Bur against the Er Galatians, 17 German, 176 gerius, 177 ; German The the Smalcald Smalcald, 18 restored and writes agains at Leipsic, 1 papacy, 190 ; called as ar Mansfeld, 193 preaches at arbitrator, 19 195 ; confess Eisleben, 196 berg, 197 ; 195 and 196.

MAGDEBURG, 22

MANSFELD, city

MANSFELD, Cou 56 ; controver

MARBURG, Conf of, 155.

MARRIAGE of received, 134.

MAXIMILIAN I.,

MEISSEN, Bisho

MELANCHTHON, turn, 104 ; not Luther's mar 152 ; at Augs 169 ; funeral Luther's dea upon Luther,

"MILK and But

MINING at Möh

MILTITZ, Karl v 59 ; meets L reconcile, 77.

MÖHRA, its situ 17 ; its minin by Luther, 91.

MORAL victory.

MOTHER, Luthe Martin, 20 ; h

MÜHLHAUSEN,

MUNZER, Thon preaching, 12 128 ; killed in

N.

"New Prophets," The, 125.
New Testament, The, translated, 99; the price of, 118; prohibited by the Roman Catholic Church, 119; comments by the enemy, 119.
Nimptsch, Cloister, 133.
"Null-brothers," 22.
Nuremberg, Diet of, in 1522, 120; the religious peace of, 174; the Roman Catholic league of, 187.

O.

Ökolompad, John, 152; present at Marburg, 153; his request, 154.
Opinions upon Luther, 201–211.
Order of Church service, 122; further improved, 137; free service conceived, 137; in German, complete, 189.
Orlamünde, 124.

P.

Parental training, 20.
Paul III., Pope, 176; calls a council, 182.
Peasant War, 127; bloody scenes, 129; ended in atrocities, 131.
Persecutions against Protestants, 121.
Philip of Hesse, 85; assists the Reformation, 137; calls a conference, 151; departs from Augsburg, 169.
Pleissenburg, 63.
Pope, The, as a man, 45; his opinion of Luther, 48; cites Luther to appear, 48; supremacy of, 62; by human right, 65; confessing sins, 97.
Postils, German Church, 99.
Prayer of Luther, 142; in sickness, 183.
Protest at Spire, 159.
Protestant, Origin of the name, 159.
Prussia, 121.
Psalms, The Penitential, translated, 42.

R.

Ranke, 210.
Reformation, The, begun, 7; spreading, 66; causing disturbance, 80; radical measures of, 102; progress of, 117; in the cities, 121; retarded by the Diet of Spire (1529), 159; by dissensions on the Lord's Supper, 180; introduced in Halle, Brunswick, Cologne, 191.
Regensburg, Diet of, 189.
Reichenbach, Philip, 133.
Reinecke, Hans, 22.
Relics at Wittenberg, 15; at Halle, 97.
Repentance, the first thesis, 14.
Reuchlin, John, 44; on Luther, 46.
Rome, 37; its churches and clergy, 38; the true Babylon, 45.
Rose, The Golden, 58.

S.

Sacramentarians, The, 151.
Sacraments, 75.
Satan on the Wartburg, 96.
Sayings, Luther's bold, 84; at Worms, 88; at Friedberg, 90; on Duke George, 106.
Scala Sancta, 38.
Schalbean College, 24.
Schauenburg, Sylvester von, 70.
Scholastic learning, at Erfurt, 25; neglects Bible study, 39.
Schools and schoolmasters, 21; asked for, 74; urgently demanded, 123.
Schwabach Articles, 157.
Sickengen, Franz von, 70; offers a refuge to Luther, 84.
Sins classified and paid for, 13.
Smalcald, The League of, 172; the Articles of, 182; the League defeated, 199.
Spalatin, 56; warns Luther, 84; his account of Luther's seizure, 95.
Spire, Diet of, (1526), 139; another in 1529, 158; a third in 1544, 190.
Squire George, 94.
St. Ann, 29.
Staupitz, John von, 31; advises Luther, 33; recommends him, 35; urges him, 39; at Augsburg, 54; retires to Salzburg, 80.
Stolberg, 211.
Stotternheim, 29.
St. Peter's Church, 39; built by indulgences, 10.
Students, The, and Luther at Jena, 109–114.
Swan Legend, 68.

T.

Tauler, John, 41; his influence upon Luther, 42.
Tetzel, John 9; his origin, 11; indulgence preacher and inquisitor, 12; his appearance and manner of work, 12; issues counter-theses, 47; dies of chagrin, 59.
Teutonic Knights, The, 121.
Theses, Luther's, 8; the first on repentance, 14; read all over Germany, 15; met by the Church, 43; sent to the Pope, 44; variously received, 46.
Torgau, The city of, 162.
Torgau, Articles of, 162.
Trebonius, John, 24.
Trent, Council of, called, 190; convenes, 191.
Treves, Archbishop of, 60; negotiates with Luther, 90.
Tribulation, the Christian's lot, 15.
Trutvetter, Jodokus, 25.
Turks, The, used as a pretext, 10; the genuine kind of, 49; Luther writes against them, 158; begin war against Austria, 173.

U.

UNION, refused at Marburg, 155 ; attempted at Schwabach, 157 ; accomplished at Wittenberg, 181.
USURY and usurers, 187.

V.

VEHEMENCE of Luther, 143 ; explained by himself, 144 ; by Erasmus, 197.
VERGERIUS visits Wittenberg, 177 ; interview with Luther, 178 ; becomes a Protestant, 179.
VIRGIN MARY, The, 29 ; prayed to, 42.

W.

WARTBURG Castle, 92 ; the refuge of Luther, 93.
WEDDING, Luther's, 134 ; rings and gifts, 134.

WIEGAND, 24.
WIELAND, 211.
WITTENBERG, City of, 36 ; troubles at, 101 ; plague in, 146.
WITTENBERG, University of, founded, 36 ; takes Luther's part, 47 ; crowded with students, 101 ; temporarily removed to Jena, 146 ; united with Halle, 191.
WITTENBERG Concord, The, 181.
WORMS, Diet of, 82 ; the grand assemblage, 86.

Z.

ZWICKAU, City of, 103.
ZWICKAU, Prophets of, 103 ; treatment of, by Luther, 117.
ZWINGLI, 151 ; his view of the Lord's Supper, 152 ; disputes with Luther, 153.